"I'm glad I ran into you, Paige," Josh said.

"Why?" Paige asked apprehensively. She leaned back against the clammy brick wall of P3's alley.

"Because," Josh continued, leaning in. His voice got deeper, almost robotic. And his face began to change too, darkening into a sinister glower. Paige could feel his breath—hot and fetid—gust onto her face. "You've got my heart."

Paige glanced down and saw Josh's hand reaching toward her chest. His arm was shaking, as if infused with some sort of electricity. And as his fingertips brushed the bare skin above the low-cut bodice of her dress, his nails instantly grew into glinting, razorlike talons.

In fact, his entire hand transformed into a metallic, clawlike, lethal weapon.

D1011844

Charmed™

Published by Simon & Schuster

DATE WITH DEATH

An original novel by Elizabeth Lenhard

Based on the hit TV series created by

Constance M. Burge

SIMON PULSE

New York London Toronto Sydney Singapore

For Allison, Cathy, Jen, Rachel and Reva

If you purchased this book without a cover, you should be aware that this book is stolen property. It was reported as "unsold and destroyed" to the publisher, and neither the author nor the publisher has received any payment for this "stripped book."

This book is a work of fiction. Any references to historical events, real people, or real locales are used fictitiously. Other names, characters, places, and incidents are the product of the author's imagination, and any resemblance to actual events or locales or persons, living or dead, is entirely coincidental.

First Simon Pulse edition September 2002
™ & © 2002 Spelling Television Inc. All Rights Reserved.

SIMON PULSE
An imprint of Simon & Schuster
Children's Publishing Division
1230 Avenue of the Americas
New York, NY 10020

All rights reserved, including the right of
reproduction in whole or in part in any form.

The text of this book was set in Palatino.

Printed in the United States of America

2   4   6   8   10   9   7   5   3   1

Library of Congress Control Number 2002107164

ISBN 0-689-85078-6

I'd like to thank Alice La Plante and Clare La Plante, authors of *Dear Saint Anne, Send Me a Man: And Other Time-Honored Prayers for Love* (Universe Publishing, New York). There are many versions of St. Catherine's tale floating around. The one I found in the La Plantes' whimsical book inspired this story.

Chapter

1

Phoebe Halliwell sank into a chair at her favorite coffeehouse—City Drip.

Man, she thought, taking a big slurp of her grandé Chai latte and glancing around the shabby-chic joint, *I haven't been in here in forever.*

Actually she hadn't been there since she graduated from college. Back when she'd been a student, Phoebe had been a part of the wallpaper at City Drip. She'd set up camp at this window-side table with her books and sketch pad and a steady supply of caffeine. Occasionally she'd take a break to pay attention to some dreadlocked and disenchanted singer-songwriter strumming an acoustic guitar in the corner. Or she'd check out the latest really bad art for sale. If she got *really* bored, San Francisco's coolest neighborhood—Haight-Ashbury—was right outside the door. A twenty-minute powershop and she'd be back at work.

When you think about it, she thought, *I owe my degree to this place.*

Phoebe rolled her eyes as she remembered what a struggle college had been. It was weird because her older sister, Piper, had been a total smarty-pants—okay, let's face it, a nerd—in high school. Now, she was an on-top-of-it-all business owner, running their nightclub, P3. Phoebe's younger sister, Paige, was also a bit of a brainiac—or at least extremely driven—working to save the world as an assistant at a child welfare clinic. And then there was her late sister, Prue, who'd been a studious art historian before branching into photography.

But book smarts had *never* been Phoebe's bag. She'd taken a few classes during her post high–school years in New York. Then, after moving back to San Francisco to live with her sisters, she'd bounced from job to job for a while, before finally settling down and snagging her B.A. That is, after logging in about a thousand hours at City Drip.

And now, here I am again—hitting the books, Phoebe thought, taking another spicy sip of Chai and glaring at the reading she'd brought to the coffeehouse. She sifted through the stack of super-thick tomes and sighed.

"Let's see," she muttered. "We've got *Contemporary Bride*, *Blushing Bride*, and the oh-so-classy *Getting Hitched*. Where to begin?"

Phoebe grabbed *Blushing Bride* and opened it up to an advertisement featuring several sheepish-looking models in fluffy, lime green bridesmaid's dresses.

"Okay, *moving* on!" Phoebe whispered, grabbing *Contemporary Bride*. The first article she happened upon advised brides to include pressed rose petals in the envelope of every "Save-the-Date" card.

Save-the-Date cards? Phoebe thought. *I didn't know about "Save-the-Date" cards! I don't know if I can even get it together to send out invitations. And now when I do, nobody will have saved the date! There will be no wedding guests! My big day—ruined!*

Phoebe slumped back in her chair and stared gloomily out the window. The thing was, she had a hard time thinking of her wedding day in a few months as her "big day"! It wasn't that she didn't absolutely adore her fiancé, Cole. And she'd even gotten over her fear of becoming a vanilla-flavored, happy housewife the minute she uttered the words, "I do."

But the whole white wedding thing? Phoebe just had a hard time buying into it.

I guess that's what comes from growing up in an . . . um, slightly unconventional family, Phoebe thought with a little smile. *I mean, we are witches.*

Phoebe's mind flashed back to the fateful day that she'd discovered she was a witch. It had happened in the attic of Halliwell Manor, the rambling Victorian mansion where Phoebe and her older sisters had grown up. Nosing around one day, Phoebe had discovered the magical Book of Shadows and unwittingly uttered a spell that unleashed the sisters' magical powers. And not just any magical powers. The Halliwells were the Charmed Ones—supernatural whizzes on their own but almost unconquerable when they banded together as a trio.

That would be the good old Power of Three, Phoebe mused.

Ever since that day Phoebe had been having premonitions. These visions of the future sent the sisters on wild goose chases to save innocents and vanquish demons, warlocks, and whatever other baddies came along to try to conquer the Power of Three. Piper had learned to freeze time or blow things up with the flick of a finger.

Along the way Piper had married Leo, despite the fact that he was the sisters' Whitelighter—an angel assigned by the Elders to protect them. Witch-Whitelighter romances were totally frowned upon in the Elders' world. But somehow Leo and Piper's love had managed to beat the odds.

Meanwhile Phoebe had fallen head over heels for Cole, an assistant district attorney who happened to be moonlighting as Belthazor, a high-level demon intent on doing in the

Charmed Ones. (Not that Phoebe knew this at the time, of course.) Once Cole fell for Phoebe, though, he'd said *sayonara* to the evil underworld. In fact he'd risked life and limb to do so. Eventually he'd even given up his powers, becoming a full-fledged human being.

And finally, Phoebe thought with a stab of grief, the worst had happened. The Source of all evil had sent an assassin to kill the Charmed Ones. After years of misses, he'd made a successful hit. Prue was killed, destroying the Power of Three.

Temporarily, of course. Because that was when Paige—who would be the love child of the girls' mother and *her* Whitelighter—turned up. After that, their big, Victorian house became home to a new set of Charmed Ones. Paige discovered that, just like Leo, she had the Whitelighter's ability to orb—to disappear in a flurry of shimmery, sparks of light. She could also orb objects into her hand.

Even without all our magic and save-the-world destinies and such, Phoebe thought, *our family's never been normal in the marital department. I mean, Mom left Dad for her Whitelighter before passing away when we were little. And while our grandmother was raising us, she somehow found the time to marry and divorce six times. And let's not forget that Piper and Leo's wedding was almost ruined when Prue's astral projection went wild and was accused of murder.*

But in the end, Leo and Piper did have a dreamy wedding, Phoebe remembered with a happy sigh.

So why can't I? she thought. *I mean, just because I'm not a domestic goddess like my big sister, does that mean I can't pull off a dream wedding? Would it be so—*

"Unbelievable!"

Phoebe gave a start and looked up. *Well, well,* she thought. *If it isn't my favorite sorority sisters.*

The two women bearing down on Phoebe in a gust of Happy perfume and sparkling lip gloss had been in a couple of her classes at school. Not that learning had been even close to the top of their to-do lists. They were more interested in gossiping about guys and trying to suck Phoebe into their dish sessions.

"Phoebe Halliwell!" Missy, the tall, skinny one, cried.

"Where have you *been*?" squealed the other one, a buxom blonde named Carla.

"Um, home?" Phoebe said. "After that whole graduation thing, I decided to stop hanging around those classes."

"Phoebe! Always with a joke," Carla said, plopping into the empty chair at Phoebe's table. Missy dragged over a third chair and squeezed in.

By all means, Phoebe thought dryly, *have a seat.*

"I guess you missed the Drip," Missy said.

"Well, I was just looking for a place to do some reading," Phoebe said. "You know, a *quiet* place?"

"Oh! My! God!" Carla shrieked, pointing at Phoebe's left hand.

Oh-kay, Phoebe thought, *guess she missed that memo about* the quiet.

"Is that an engagement ring on your finger?" Carla continued.

"Um, yup, that would be my rock," Phoebe said, sheepishly, glancing at the sparkly ring Cole had given her. "I'm getting married in a few months."

"Awwwww, you are *so* lucky!" Missy gushed. "Tell us about him."

"Oh, well, let's just say Cole is a . . . really old soul," Phoebe said with a secret smile. It was no lie. Cole had been a demon for a couple centuries before giving it all up for her.

"And I love him," Phoebe continued simply.

"Oh, what I wouldn't give," Carla said. She grabbed one of Phoebe's bridal magazines and flipped a few pages with a long, pink fingernail. "I'm *so* single. And here it is, February second and I still don't have a date for Valentine's Day. But I just signed up for Kiss.com. You know, the Internet dating service? I'm hoping that's gonna be, like, a total turning point for me in the romance department!"

"Great!" Phoebe said, scooping up her magazines and feeling grateful that she'd gotten her Chai in a to-go cup. "Good luck with that. But you know, girls, I just remembered I have to be someplace in ten minutes. It was great to see you!"

"You too!" Missy and Carla trilled.

"You have to call us for lunch," Carla said. "We'll dish about blushers and bustles and stuff!"

Okay, forget Save-the-Date cards, Phoebe thought, feeling another wave of panic wash over her. *What the heck is a blusher?*

She gave the girls a weak wave and rushed out of the coffeehouse.

Oh, she worried as she hurried down Haight Street. *Maybe I'm just not bride material!*

Ugh, I am such *the little wife*, Piper thought in disgust. She was standing at the island in the Manor's kitchen. Normally it was her favorite room in the house with its bright white beadboard and sturdy, oak table.

Yeah, we got the strongest one in the store after the last one was destroyed by yet another demon, Piper thought, rolling her eyes. *I don't know why our unholy invaders always have to land in my kitchen! Like last week, that primordial demon came to visit and totally gunked up my Kitchen-Aid mixer when I exploded him.*

Piper caught herself midthought and rolled her eyes.

"Okay, stressing about my mixer? That just proves it," she muttered to herself. "I *am* Harriet Nelson. And appropriately enough, here I am making meatloaf, green beans, and mashed potatoes for dinner. My husband even served in World War II!"

Piper sighed as she popped the ends off a handful of green beans and tossed them into a bowl. She remembered what it had been like when she and Leo had first gotten married. She was so eager to please that she'd made him elaborate spreads of sushi and sake; homemade pasta and tiramisu, raspberry sorbet and six-layer cakes—the works.

And Leo, sweetie that he was, never said anything but "thank you." But eventually she'd realized that her hubbie was never more enthusiastic than when she made meals that looked like his childhood . . . in the 1930s. That meant meat and potatoes.

So, dutiful dame that she was, she was making meat and potatoes for dinner tonight.

Again.

It wasn't that Piper didn't like cooking for the family. In fact she was never happier than when she was whipping up a meal. After all, she'd been a chef before she opened up P3. In fact the first time she'd ever accidentally used her freezing power had been to remedy a botched recipe during a tryout for a job in a restaurant kitchen.

But lately she'd been feeling a bit frumpy compared to her younger sisters. Phoebe, she of the perma-tan and blonde-streaked shiny locks only had to get her skinny self out of bed in the morning to look glam. And Paige . . . *well, let's just say I am still getting used to having a sister who looks like Snow White—all creamy pale skin, black hair, and puckery, glossed lips. She makes me feel like such the . . . eldest sister!*

"Hi, Ma! What's for dinner?"

Piper started and looked up. Paige was sauntering into the kitchen with a grin on her face.

You know, Piper thought, *these retro greetings of Paige's aren't helping me feel any more hip. It's either the "Hi, Ma," line or "Honey, I'm home!" Or, what was it she said yesterday at breakfast? "Gee whiz, that's great coffee!"*

Piper sighed. She knew Paige didn't mean to tease her. It was just there was no denying their relationship still had some rough edges. Piper couldn't stand Paige's bohemian decorating style, for instance. And the way she tossed her clothes, books, whatever, on the closest piece of furniture—oooh, that drove Piper nuts.

But Piper knew Paige was still struggling to fit into her new life as a Halliwell . . . and a witch. So she tried to cut her sis some slack.

"Um, meatloaf, Biff!" Piper said brightly, trying not to cringe as Paige tossed her briefcase onto the kitchen table. "Green beans, potatoes . . ."

"Again?" Paige asked.

"Again," Piper said, looking down and pursing her lips. "Yeah, I guess I'm in a bit of a rut."

"I was kidding," Paige said, rolling her huge, hazel eyes and hopping up to take a seat on the counter. She grabbed a potato and knife and started peeling. "C'mon, I was a vegetarian before I moved in here. Your meatloaf totally converted me back to being a carnivore."

"Thanks," Piper said, flashing Paige a smile. "But, you know, I think I do need to shake things up a bit. I've been a ball-and-chain for, wow, more than a year now."

"Oh, please, you and Leo are total mush-pots," Paige said. "I see you smooching when-ever one of us leaves the room."

"If you've left the room, how have you seen it, Paige?" Piper said. She felt her cheeks go hot.

"Well, I might have . . . left the room slowly once," Paige said with a sheepish grin. "Whatever. My point is, I would give anything to be all married and settled."

"Really?" Piper said in surprise. "You, the Saturday Night Fever of P3? I've seen you dance with dozens of different guys at the club."

"Yeah, but hardly any of them stick around after the dance," Paige complained. "They're just fly-by-night hotties. Gorgeous and buff and adoring, yes. But do any of them bring me chicken soup when I have a cold?"

"I just never pegged you as the chicken soup type," Piper said, suppressing a smile as she put a pot of water on the stove to boil.

"Yeah, I always think of borscht when it comes to Paige."

The sisters glanced at the kitchen doorway.

Phoebe was standing there with an armload of bridal magazines and a grin.

"Or . . . hmm, maybe beef barley," Phoebe added.

"Consommé!" Piper chimed in with a nod.

"Okay, okay," Paige said, tossing her peeled potato at Piper. "I get your point. So maybe I'm not so domestic. But would it be so wrong if I had a boyfriend who'd say . . . bring me roses on Valentine's Day?"

"Aha," Phoebe said, crossing over to the island and heaving her thick stack of magazines onto the counter with a bang. "That's what this is about. It's February second. You're angsting about Valentine's."

"Well, how can I not?" Paige protested, grabbing another potato. "I mean, Piper and Leo are all but knocked up."

"Hello!" Piper squealed. "I am *not* pregnant, thank you very much."

As she said this, Piper felt a little pang. Because it was true. She and Leo had been talking about having a baby for a while now. But talking and . . . conceiving? Well, that was a big leap. Especially when demons dropped into your kitchen on a weekly basis. At the moment they were still at an impasse, and Piper was the one who couldn't budge. She'd gone through so many huge changes lately, it was hard for her to sign onto anther one. So Operation Baby was definitely on hold. No matter how much Leo protested.

"Okay, but you could be," Paige said. "You're legal and in love. And Phoebe's shopping for blushers, for Pete's sake."

"Okay, *what* is a blusher?" Phoebe sputtered. "How does everyone know these things?"

"My point is, I'm at square one," Paige wailed. "I have no boyfriend. No prospects. No plans this Saturday. I'm in such a dry spell!"

"Paige, honey," Piper said gently, "didn't you have a date, like, three days ago?"

Well . . . yeah, but he was wearing the worst shoes," Paige replied. "So obviously he was *not* boyfriend material."

Shoes? Piper thought. *Okay, clearly Paige and I have different criteria when it comes to men.*

"The guys I date are so random," Paige continued. "I mean, take that guy I met on the streetcar a few weeks ago. I thought we had a connection but once I got to know him, I realized—*poof*—we had nothing in common."

"Well, c'mon Paige," Piper said. "You *had* to know that was a stretch! His name was Lung Chow and he barely spoke English!"

Paige giggled.

"I guess you're right," she said. "I wish I could, you know, shop for men the way you shop for clothes. When you're in a store, you only try on the outfits you think might fit, right? But when you're dating, you have to commit to dinner and a movie with that outfit. And before you even get to the soup, you realize, that's a size twenty-two, orange sweater! That won't fit me at all!"

"Okay, you completely lost me with the metaphor there," Piper said with a laugh. But out of the corner of her eye, she saw Phoebe perk up.

"You need a kiss!" Phoebe declared to Paige.

"Phoebe, please," Paige said. "This is not about necking with some hottie. I'm talking about trying to find love! But I guess kissing wouldn't hurt . . ."

"Not that kind of kiss," Phoebe said. "I just ran into some people who told me about Kiss.com. It's a Web site where you . . . shop for men! Just like you said."

"Like . . . personal ads?" Paige said, curling her lip. "Isn't that a little desperate?"

"And Lung Chow from the streetcar isn't?" Phoebe retorted. "Heck, I think it sounds fun. If I were single, I'd go for it."

"Go for what?" said a rumbly voice from the back door. It was Cole, who had just slipped into the kitchen from the garage. He winked at Phoebe and said, "Hello, wife-to-be. So . . . go for what?"

"Go for . . . some meatloaf, I *really* could," Phoebe covered quickly. She hopped over to Cole and gave him a kiss on the cheek. Then she turned to Piper. "So what else is for dinner, Ma? I'm starving."

"Not you too!" Piper said, mock-scowling at

her sister and tossing a dinner roll at her. The roll was halfway across the room when Leo orbed in, catching the flying bread right in the eye.

"Yeow!" he cried, rubbing his head painfully. "I put in a hard day of work in the heavens and this is the homecoming I get?"

"You got it, sweetie," Piper said, trotting over to plant a quick kiss on his lips. "*And* you get meatloaf for dinner."

"Great!" Leo said, barely concealing his relief.

Oh yeah, I'm Harriet Nelson all right, Piper thought as she started setting the table. *But I guess it could be worse. I could be surfing for dates on Kiss.com.*

I can't *believe I'm surfing for dates on Kiss.com*, Paige thought with a moan. She was clicking away at the Halliwell computer, which was stashed on Grams's old Victorian desk in the kitchen. The fact that she was bloated from too much mashed potatoes didn't help matters. She heaved a big sigh.

"Okay," Paige muttered as she scrolled through picture after picture, "these pickings are way slim. Here's a picture of . . . Nigel, who desperately needs a green card, not to mention some orthodontia. And then there's Nathan. A mouth-breather, I can just tell. And, whoa, how many chins does *that* dude have? The jpeg's kind of fuzzy but I think I see . . . four?

"This is *definitely* not as fun as shopping,"
Paige continued. "What a bunch of lo—hel-*lo*!
Who's this?"

Paige was feasting her eyes on a hottie with a
head full of soft brown curls, a Matt Damon
grin, and broad shoulders. The screen name next
to the picture was, "Just James."

Well . . . maybe I'll give Kiss.com a try after all,
Paige said with a little grin. She opened the computer scanner and slipped in a picture of herself.
In the snapshot she was winking and wearing
her favorite, skimpy halter top.

"Okay, so it's a little over the top," Paige murmured   as   the   cheesecake   shot   suddenly
appeared on her computer screen. "But it *is* a
competitive market!"

Next, Paige clicked the POST AN AD button and
dashed off a quick paragraph:

"Me? A caffeine addict with a dry wit, a closet
full of high heels, a stereo set too loud, and a
passion for my work. You? You know a fine wine
and you can make a girl laugh. You don't smoke,
but you do dance. You treat your mother right.
And when it comes to the love of your life?
You're looking for a little magic."

"Truer than you know, boys," Paige said
wryly. "Well, let's see what happens."

And with that, she moved her cursor to the
SEND button and gave it an adamant click.

Chapter

2

"At laaasst, my looooove is here to stay . . ."

Paige was stuck in traffic in her VW bug, glaring at the radio.

Lovely, she thought. *I had a totally stressful day at the clinic trying to place a kid in foster care. Now I'm jammed neck-deep in traffic. And the music is mocking me. My love isn't here to stay. I have no love. I'm like Bridget Jones without the British accent.*

She switched to her favorite jazz station. She could always count on that for some awesome Charlie Parker.

"Someday he'll come along . . ." crooned a silky woman's voice. "The man I looooove . . ."

"Whatever!" Paige sputtered, clicking the radio off. "I swear, Valentine's Day is still two weeks away. Isn't this a little excessive?"

Paige sighed as she finally turned off the crammed main drag onto her own street. She parked in front of Halliwell Manor and stomped up the steps to the front door. She was *that* close to slamming it on her way in but stopped herself at the last moment.

Hmmm . . . I just realized I don't yet know the door-slamming policy at Halliwell Manor, she thought. *Does Piper hate it? Does it give Phoebe a migraine? Does Phoebe get migraines?*

Paige shook her head as she made a beeline for the kitchen.

I'm still getting used to this strangers-as-sisters thing, she thought.

Speaking of which, there was Piper at the kitchen computer.

"Hi," Piper called, waving distractedly as Paige slumped against the counter. "I'm looking for some new recipes. Something . . . exciting, yet totally traditional. You think that exists?"

"Sounds like a stretch to me," Paige said with a shrug.

"You're probably right," Piper said, rolling her eyes. "So how was your day at the office, Biff?"

"Oh, the usual—attempts to create social change. Failure to create social change," Paige joked. She forced herself to smile. "Thanks for asking, by the way. I mean, since singletons are supposed to be invisible this month."

"Excuse me?" Piper said, tearing her eyes

from the computer screen to scrutinize Paige. "What are you talking about?"

"It's February, remember?" Paige complained. "Everywhere you go, red and pink! Love songs on every station. Couples nuzzling each other in supermarkets. Ew."

"Oh," Piper said, glancing back at the computer. "So I guess it's safe to say you haven't been kissed?"

"Oh, you mean Kiss.com?" Paige said. She felt a flutter of anxiety in her stomach. Ever since she'd put her picture on the site two nights ealier, she'd regretted it.

"Well, I haven't exactly checked back in," she admitted.

"Okay, why?" Piper said gently.

"I'm just sure it's going to be depressing!" Paige admitted, pulling a chair away from the kitchen table and plopping down next to Piper. "I mean, I wrote a note to this one guy—Just James. But what if he didn't write back? What if he found me repulsive?"

"Repulsive?" Piper asked. Paige could tell she was suppressing a laugh. "Yeah, that's gonna happen. But on the other hand, so what if he does? Maybe some other guy who's a whole lot better than Just James has spotted *you*."

"Okay, that's the other thing," Paige said. "Suppose some guys write to me. And they're all a bunch of dweebs. Then I learn that . . . I attract dweebs. Or jerks. Or comic-reading, strange-smelling supergeeks. I'm not sure if I'm ready to learn that those kinds of guys are my type."

As Paige finished her outburst, she bit her lip. She knew she was being irrational. In fact, she was regretting every word that had just come out of her mouth. Until Piper reacted in a way that was downright . . . sisterly.

"Paige," Piper said, reaching over to smooth down a tousled lock of Paige's black hair. "Believe me, you are not the dweeb type. Unreliable rock-and-roll dudes, maybe."

Paige had to laugh. Piper had her pegged.

"But that's only because you're so cool," Piper continued. "Now I'm going to make you some herbal tea and you are going to sit down and log onto Kiss.com. I'm *sure* it's not going to be as bad as all that."

Paige grinned gratefully as Piper stood up and prodded her into the desk chair.

"You better watch it," she said to Piper. "A girl could get used to this big sister routine."

"Count on it," Piper said with her typical sweet bluntness. Then she pointed at the computer's mouse. "Now start pointing and clicking. I'll brew up the Tension Tamer."

Paige laughed as she typed in the Web site's address. Then she keyed in her password and held her breath. A window popped up.

"You've been kissed with forty-three messages," it read.

"Whoa!" Paige exclaimed. "Um, Piper . . . you better make that an extra-large tea. I think I'm going to be here for a while."

An hour later, Paige was still responding to her eager e-suitors.

Some of the first responses had been . . . discouraging.

"Hey, Sugar Lips," wrote a guy called Blue-Eyed Babe. "U are 2 cute. Let's get together."

"Ick!" Paige had cried. "Delete, delete, delete."

Then there was the math professor who wrote her a numeric love ode. And the dude who might have been pretty hot, 250 pounds ago.

But then she clicked on a note from . . . Just James! He sounded totally nice and had asked her to meet him for coffee the next day.

And after Just James, things only got better. Piper had been right. So far Paige had made dates with an E.R. doctor with sandy blond hair and incredibly white teeth. A public-aid lawyer whose politics were identical to Paige's. And a surfer who wrote poetry.

Now Paige was reading a profile of a whimsical ice-cream entrepreneur.

"Sure, Rocky Road," Paige typed quickly. "Why don't we get together. How's . . ."

Paige paused to check her Palm Pilot. Her calendar was getting sort of crammed. But Rocky Road was just too cute to resist.

". . . lunch on Thursday?" she typed.

As she hit SEND, she blinked. A quick spasm of light had shot out of the computer. It was so quick, she almost thought it was her imagination.

"Huh," she muttered as she clicked on the next guy's e-mail. This one was a veterinarian with red curls and green eyes and five brothers and sisters.

"This is too good to be true," Paige muttered as she typed, "Coffee, tomorrow night?" Then she moved her cursor to the send button.

Click. (Flash.)

"It keeps doing that," Paige said, shaking her head to clear the spots from her eyes. "I wonder if something's wrong with the computer. I'll have to remember to mention it to Piper. . . . Ooh, who's this one? A fellow social worker? Be still my heart."

Click. (Flash.)

Paige wended her way through almost all forty-three of her messages before she called it quits.

"I'll have to come back for the rest," she yawned, moving the mouse to send off her last response.

Click. (Flash.)

She shook her head blearily and stood up. Instantly she felt a wave of dizziness swoop through her head.

"Whoa," she whispered, grabbing the desk

chair for support. She stood still for a moment and tried to shake the fog out of her brain.

"I guess all that admiration went to my head," she said. Then, as the dizziness passed, she giggled.

Immediately Piper and Phoebe poked their heads into the kitchen.

"Do I hear laughter?" Piper said. "As in success?"

"So!" Paige said, thrusting her Palm Pilot out to them. "Check it out. I'm booked solid for the next week. Lunch dates, coffee dates, dinners, drinks. I'm, like, the prom queen of Kiss.com."

"I think I created a monster," Piper said, gaping at the crowded calendar page on Paige's Palm Pilot. "You really want to date all these guys?"

"It's called playing the field," Phoebe said with a smile. "I used to do it all the time."

"I remember," Piper said dryly. "And that was before they invented the Palm Pilot. Remember when those two guys, both named Jeff, showed up for a date at the same time?"

"Those were the days," Phoebe said dreamily.

Paige winked at her and then turned to grin at Piper.

"Don't you worry," Paige said. "I've got a grip. I'll just check these guys out and then narrow it down to, oh, three or four with real potential."

"Three or four?!" said a voice behind her. Paige whipped around to see Leo, leaning against the kitchen doorjamb. "You're going to date three or four men at the same time? Isn't that a little . . . fast?"

"Leo," Phoebe squealed. "There's nothing *wrong* with it. Might I remind you, it's the twenty-first century. Women work now, and we vote and we date."

"I'm well aware," Leo said dryly. "I'm married to a lady business owner, aren't I?"

"*Lady* business owner?" Piper protested. "What am I? Mary Kay?"

"Oh-kay," Paige said, stepping between her sister and brother-in-law. "I'd love to listen to this oh-so-retro repartee, but I have to get ready. My first date is dinner in, oh, about two hours."

"You're kidding!" Piper said. "Paige, I think Leo's right. That's fast!"

"Don't listen to them," Phoebe said, slinging an arm around Paige's shoulders. "I think it's great! In fact, I'm going to help you get ready. Let me introduce you to one of the joys of being a Halliwell. You get to raid your sister's closet before a big date."

"You read my mind," Paige said with a grin as she followed Phoebe out of the kitchen. As she climbed the stairs to Phoebe's bedroom, she found herself cheerfully humming a familiar tune.

"At laaaaast," she sang softly, "my loooove is here to stay."

• • •

Piper watched Paige and Phoebe trot out of the kitchen. Then she turned to grin at her husband.

"I guess love is in the air," she said, slipping into his arms and planting a kiss on the tip of his nose.

"Do you ever miss being single?" Leo said, gazing into Piper's eyes and smoothing a lock of hair off her forehead. "Being picked up at the door? Being taken out by a guy who isn't, um, dead and can, say, pick up the dinner check?"

Piper laughed and gave Leo another kiss.

"Not for a minute," she said sweetly. "Who wants to date when you can be married to an angel? And besides, I told you I was never beating the boys off with sticks."

"That's only because those fellas were too dumb to see how special you are," Leo said. His green eyes crinkled at the corners as he smiled at his wife. "Lucky for me."

Piper felt a warm and gooey sensation spread through her. She and Leo hadn't had a mushy conversation like this in so long!

"No, I'm the one who's lucky," she said, snuggling up against his strong chest.

"So what's for dinner?" Leo asked, rubbing her back idly.

Piper started.

Oh-kay, she thought. *Enough with the goo. Ozzie Nelson is back.* She pushed Leo away and shrugged.

"Yeah," she said dryly. "I was just looking up some recipes. I'll get right on that."

"Piper," Leo said, catching her elbow. "Did I say something wrong?"

"Noooo," Piper said. "You were just . . . being a husband, that's all."

Leo's worried face relaxed again.

"You got it," he said sweetly. "And you're my wife. Just the way I want it."

Piper smiled weakly and turned to the computer as Leo wandered out of the kitchen. She sighed as she started to type in the address to the recipe Web site.

But then something caught her eye. The Internet was still tuned to Kiss.com, she realized. Hovering above a window that said, "Paige Matthews, you have eight unopened messages," was one of those flashing ad banners.

"Is your relationship in a rut?" the ad read. "Do you and your mate have what it takes to go the distance? Do you care enough to find out?"

"Can you say manipulative?" Piper muttered, rolling her eyes. She started to click back to her recipe page, but something made her drag the cursor over to the ad.

"Just curious . . ." she whispered as she clicked on it. Suddenly she was gazing at a busy Web site filled with urgently bouncing hearts and pulsing hotlinks. The Web site's name flashed at the top of the screen.

"Women are Cats, Men are Dogs," Piper read out loud. "Well, that sort of makes sense . . ." Then her eye fell on a link.

"Humdrum husband?" it read. "Our relationship regimen will snap that marriage back into shape."

Hmmm, Piper thought, casually clicking on the link. The screen filled with a list of about a dozen quizzes, exercises, and games you could play to raise your consciousness and jump-start your marriage.

"Oh, please," Piper said to herself. "That's so Oprah. But then again . . . Oprah is really popular!"

Before Piper knew it she was printing out a stack of quizzes and questionnaires.

"Why not?" she said to herself blithely. "It's not like Leo and I have to take these things seriously. It'll be fun!"

Phoebe could dimly hear Paige's voice, but she couldn't understand a word she was saying.

"Wait a minute," Phoebe said, awkwardly extricating herself from the crowded depths of her walk-in closet. She was holding a very short, green leather skirt in one hand and a gauzy black sweater in the other. She tossed them to Paige, who was sitting on the bed amongst a stack of other sexy date clothes. "I couldn't hear you."

"I said, you seem more excited about this date than I am!" Paige said. She grinned as she pawed through Phoebe's filmy clothes.

"Oh," Phoebe said, pausing for a moment. Was there a kernel of truth to that? Why *was* she so into Paige's swinging single thing?

Phoebe shook the question out of her head and smiled brightly. "Just trying to be supportive. You know, I'm new to this whole big sister thing. It's kind of fun!"

"It *is* fun!" Paige said, eyeing a transparent tank top with a raised eyebrow. "I only hope Josh Skilling provides as good a time."

Phoebe froze. "Did you just say Josh Skilling?" she asked slowly.

"Yeah, why?" Paige asked. She stared at Phoebe and her face fell. "You know him! It's all over your face. Oh, no, tell me. Is he a jerk? A freak? Am I in for the worst night of my life? Give it to me straight, doc."

"No, no, he's not a freak. . . ." Phoebe said, feeling her giddiness evaporate like a potion that had gone *poof*. "And he wasn't a jerk. Not until right before we broke up."

"What?" Paige said. Her white skin went even paler. "You're telling me that my Kiss.com date is your ex?"

"Um, yeah," Phoebe said quietly, flopping onto the bed next to Paige. "That about sums it up."

"I'm canceling," Paige said, jumping off the bed and stalking across the room to the phone. "Dating your sister's ex is completely taboo."

"No, wait," Phoebe heard herself say. She tried to act breezy. "Please, Paige. I'm engaged to Cole. Why should I care? And besides, I was the one who broke up with Josh."

"Okay, then why are you all trembly?" Paige retorted. She planted her fists on her hips and stared at Phoebe.

"I'm not, I swear," Phoebe said with a little laugh. A . . . trembly, little laugh. Paige stared her down.

"All right, I'll tell you the whole deal," Phoebe agreed. "Josh and I dated for a few months about five years ago and, at first, everything was blissville."

"And then what?" Paige said, sinking to a seat on the floor. She folded her legs beneath her and gazed up at Phoebe. "He cheated? Stood you up? Stopped calling?"

"No . . ." Phoebe said. "He just changed. It was like, all of a sudden, he couldn't quite look at me anymore. He got sort of distant and sullen. I tried to talk to him about it, you know, see if he was going through something he wasn't telling me about. But he completely shut me out. And he didn't show any signs of changing. Finally I didn't feel like I had any choice but to break up with him."

"Ugh!" Paige said. "Men are so weird!"

"Yup," Phoebe said, trying to ignore the tension roiling in her stomach. She started to return her attention to Paige's date outfit, but she paused. Then she looked at her sister.

"Doesn't it seem like everyone has one relationship that they just can't figure out? Where it went wrong? What could have been?" she said. "Well . . . Josh was mine."

"Josh?"

Phoebe started.

"Cole!" she said, staring at her fiancé leaning against the doorframe. He was wearing sweats and had a towel draped around his neck. "When did you—"

"I wasn't eavesdropping, I swear," Cole said, giving Phoebe a quick smile. "I was just heading out to the gym and was going to say good-bye. And . . . Josh?"

"Oh, Josh, shmosh," Phoebe said, grinning at Cole. "It's nothing . . ."

"He's . . . a friend?" Cole asked.

"An ex-friend," Paige piped up.

Great, Phoebe thought, *thanks for the help, sis.* It wasn't that she didn't want Cole to know about Josh. She could tell Cole anything. But talking about ex-boyfriends? Was that *ever* a good idea?

"Anyway we were trying to find the perfect outfit for Paige's date," Phoebe said, bouncing over to the bed and scooping up some shiny red pants. "What do you think of these, Cole? Would these make you interested in a woman?"

"They *did* make me interested in a woman," Cole said. "You wore those on our second date. Remember?"

Phoebe gazed at Cole with a shy smile. He remembered something like that? Cole could still surprise her.

"So who's your big date with, Paige?" Cole said, shooting Phoebe a wink.

"Oh . . . Josh," Paige said with an awkward shrug.

"Josh," Cole said. "Phoebe's friend?"

"Ex-friend," Phoebe and Paige blurted at the same time.

"Uh-huh," Cole said, giving Phoebe a hard look. "The plot thickens. I don't know what that plot is, but . . ."

"Sweetie," Phoebe said, rolling her eyes and hoping Cole wasn't going to get all macho on her. "No plot. Just ancient history."

Then she shot Paige a sly grin.

"And," Phoebe added, "maybe a new romance."

Chapter

3

Paige was on the second leg of her date with Josh Skilling—the post-dinner cocktail—and she was *not* happy. She sipped her cranberry juice-and-tonic and sighed as she watched a band gyrate wildly on P3's stage. She'd seen this group before. Chubby Hubby. They were the shimmery, poppy, slightly thrashing kind of group Paige loved. But for some reason, they weren't doing it for her tonight. She could barely wrap her brain around the music, much less get her booty shaking. She felt like her feet were glued to the floor.

Furtively she glanced at her watch.

Nine thirty-six, she thought. *Let's see, I think the last time I looked at my watch, it was 9:30. This is* not *good.*

She shot Josh Skilling a sidelong glance. Then she sighed again.

This just proves that taste in men is not DNA-driven, she thought ruefully. *I mean*, Josh *is the one that got away? The one that haunts Phoebe to this day? What's the big deal? Look at him: that wavy brown hair, bright blue eyes, chiseled jaw, broad shoulders . . . hey, wait a minute. It sounds like I was just describing a complete babe. But, for some reason, all those fabulous parts add up to zero for me.*

It must be Josh's personality that's got me bummin', Paige thought. Even though . . . the dinner conversation had been pretty cool, when she thought about it. Josh had told her hilarious stories about growing up on a farm in Ohio. And when she told him she didn't drink, he'd canceled his own order for a glass of wine. Totally sensitive.

So why was Paige yawning and yearning for an end to the night? And why, after downing a huge pile of Thai noodles, was she feeling so empty and unsatisfied?

Why, come to think of it, did she feel like she was walking through a fog?

"Do you think there was MSG in our dinner?" Paige asked Josh.

She watched his beautiful head turn toward her as if in slow-motion.

Jeez, what's with this guy, Paige thought. *He's so slow!*

"What?" Josh shouted over the music.

"MSG? In the Thai food?" Paige yelled back to him.

"MG? I guess it's a cool car," he yelled back to her. "Why do you ask? Don't tell me you only date guys with swank cars. Because I love my ancient Saab. I will give it up for no woman!"

He was funny. And charming. Paige knew this in the back of her head. But something prevented her from laughing or responding much at all. Josh's face turned hopeful.

He's waiting for me to belly up to this date, Paige thought to herself frantically. *And I'm just not up to the task. I've got to admit, if anyone's been a drip tonight, it's been me. And I have no idea why. Josh is . . . really nice. He's certainly trying to show me a good time. Why aren't I enjoying myself? What's wrong with me?*

Taking a distracted sip of her juice, she stared hard at Josh's profile. She tried to will herself to turn on the charm, touch his shoulder . . . something!

But she just stood there, motionless.

Josh must have felt her stare because he turned back to her. And for an instant, their eyes connected. Paige started. Josh's eyes almost sparkled, the way they do on cheesy TV shows. She felt a surge of energy pass between them.

At last, she thought, *a connection!*

But when Josh looked away for an instant, the spark dissipated immediately. At the same time, Chubby Hubby's last drumbeat echoed through the club and the lead singer called out, "Let's hear it for P3! We love it here, which is why we're taking a break, y'all. Back in twenty."

As the bar filled with chatter, Paige and Josh stood facing each other awkwardly. Paige opened her mouth, but somehow her entire repertoire of quips seemed to have flown out of her head. All she could lamely manage was, "Whew, what a great band. You know, I've got to get up really early tomorrow."

"Oh, me too," Josh said quickly. Paige could almost see his face slacken with relief. "But, uh . . . this was fun."

"Yeah, oh, totally," Paige said in a monotone voice.

Why even bother? she wailed inwardly. *This date was a complete bust. And to think, I have lunch, coffee, and dinner dates tomorrow.*

By the next afternoon, Paige had a theory.

She'd come up with it in the car on the way back from the most unstimulating cappuccino she'd ever drank. She blamed the man who bought her the cappuccino. Just James had been drippier than drip coffee.

But he'd been an absolute rock star compared with the simpering social worker she'd met at lunch.

Paige had finally escaped the coffee date with a limp handshake and her standard, "Don't call me, I'll call you," routine. Then she hurried to her VW and slumped into the driver's seat. She grabbed her cell phone from her purse and speed-dialed home as she turned the key in the ignition.

"I have a theory," she announced to the first person who picked up.

"Who is this?" said the voice.

"Phoebe, it's Paige," Paige said, rolling her eyes. "I thought sisters didn't have to ID themselves over the phone. I thought that was part of the whole closet-raiding, boyfriend-swapping—"

"Theory-spouting," Phoebe blurted.

"Yeah, theory-spouting package," Paige said.

"It is," Phoebe said. "But sue me, the TV was on. So spout away. What's your theory?"

"Internet dating sucks," Paige said.

"Uh-huh . . . and your theory?"

"That's it."

"Oh, honey," Phoebe said. "Give it a chance. You've only had one date—"

"Three," Paige corrected her.

"Three?" Phoebe gasped. "Paige! You're fast!"

"Thanks," Paige huffed, as she pulled into traffic and headed back to work. "I don't know what's wrong, but all these dates seem really empty. I feel like I'm only halfway there. Their jokes aren't funny. They don't look as cute as their pictures. Even the food is boring."

"That's weird," Phoebe said.

"Tell me about it," Paige said. "I mean, I am usually the first-date queen. I can spin a conversation out of nothing. But with these guys I can't think of a thing to say. I blame Kiss.com. It raises unfair expectations or something."

"I guess . . ." Phoebe said hesitantly. "So what are you gonna do?"

"What *can* I do? I've got to go on my dinner date tonight," Paige said, as she pulled into the clinic's parking lot. "It's this guy—a lawyer—named Max Wolf. I'm sure he'll be as blah as the rest, but I figure I should give it one last shot."

"That's the spirit," Phoebe said. "What are you wearing?"

"Not that it matters, but your blue capris and that little green sweater you always wear," Paige said, glancing down at her very cute outfit.

"Oh," Phoebe said flatly. "Um, did I offer you my favorite sweater?"

"Um, not exactly," Paige said with a gulp. "But I thought, you know, that whole sisterly closet-raiding thing . . ."

"Yeah, it doesn't apply to my favorite sweater, Paige," Phoebe said. Then Paige heard her sister's voice lighten. "Just do me a favor and don't spill soy sauce on it."

"Absolutely!" Paige said. "Mea culpa, Phoebs."

"And please, try to enjoy yourself," Phoebe said. "You never know, maybe this next guy will be the one!"

"The one, brought to you by Kiss.com?" Paige muttered as she clicked off her cell phone and flounced out of her car. "Fat chance."

• • •

This guy is so *the one*, Paige found herself thinking a few hours later.

She was sitting at a tiny table in an Italian restaurant, gazing at the fabulous face of Max Wolf. She was seriously smitten with him by the salad course.

Max was on the short side. And while his face was handsome, it was also a bit rugged. He looked like someone who'd been through a lot in his life.

His shiny, black hair was slicked back in a lawyerly do that Paige—she of the spiky-haired bad boyfriends—had never really liked.

In fact, objectively, Max wasn't nearly as cute as most of the Kiss.com dates she'd had. But there was something about him that captivated her.

Maybe it was his hazel eyes. They were almost yellow. And they mesmerized her. She almost couldn't take her eyes off of them as Max chatted through the meal.

"Ah," he said, peeling a leaf off a crispy Roman artichoke. "I was raised on this kind of food. Pure, authentic Italian."

"Excuse me, um, Max *Wolf*? That doesn't sound very Italian to me," Paige said with a giggle.

"Well, it's true, I'm a Jewish guy from New York City," Max said with a charming shrug. "But Paige, have you ever *had* a matzo ball? Ugh. My mother did us all a favor and put the old country recipe book in storage. Then she became a premier Italian chef. We had homemade pasta almost every night in my house."

"That's crazy!" Paige had gushed, surprising even herself with her delighted laughter. "And what did you have for dessert in your house?"

"Exactly what we're having tonight," Max said smoothly. "The best crème brûlée you ever tasted. Waiter!"

The night went on like that. Max said the perfect things and made the perfect moves. And after he drove Paige home, he walked her to the door and gave her the perfect good-night kiss.

"Wow," Max said, gazing down at Paige, his eyes sparkling a little bit in the porch light. "*You* were not what I expected to find on Kiss.com."

"You took the words right out of my mouth," Paige replied, dreamily. She closed her eyes and leaned in for another kiss.

"Why don't we take care of that on our next date," Max said softly, brushing Paige's cheek with his lips. "Will you see me again, Paige?"

"After a tease like that, I guess I'll have to," Paige joked, though her stomach was fluttering madly. "When?"

"Sunday?" Max proposed.

"You got it," Paige said. "Call me."

When she slipped quietly into the Manor, she was hit with a wave of dizziness. She stumbled back against the door and felt her chin hit her chest. After just a moment, the icky feeling passed.

Man, Paige thought, drifting across the foyer to the stairs. She couldn't seem to shake the goofy smile from her face. *That was some date!*

"Okay, Leo," Piper was saying the next morning. "Here's a good one. 'Would you compare your wife to a sycamore or an oak tree?'"

Phoebe almost choked on her toast. She was lounging in the dining room with Piper and Leo, sucking down some caffeine and waiting anxiously for Paige to come down for breakfast. She was dying to know how her date went last night with that lawyer guy. She was also dying to know that her favorite sweater made it through the evening without any stains or snags. And she was really hoping for a distraction from the old-marrieds on the other end of the table.

"This is so far from romantic, it's not even funny," Phoebe said, gnawing on her toast and gazing balefully at Piper and Leo.

"That's what I said," Leo complained. He was mushing his scrambled eggs around his plate, looking completely trapped. "Piper, these quizzes make no sense. I would never compare you to a tree. I mean, that's not very poetic, is it?"

"Well, *you're* not very poetic," Phoebe pointed out.

"Right," Leo said, before he did a double take. "Hey! Phoebe, whose side are you on?"

"Face it, Leo," Phoebe said, leaning farther

back in her chair. "You are what is known as an old-fashioned guy. A man's man. Men like you don't write poetry."

"Men like me can simply appreciate their wives without having to compare them to trees," Leo said, glaring at Piper.

But Piper ignored him and consulted the next question.

"All right then, snippy," she said. "Answer me this: 'Your wife is sick with a cold. She tells you she's fine and that you should go out with the guys and have some fun. Do you a) Happily wave good-bye and hightail it out of there? b) Say you wouldn't think of it, run her a nice bath, and make her some homemade soup? or c) Compromise by having the guys over for pizza and beer?'"

"This . . . is . . . a trick . . . question," Leo said, staring at Piper. "I'm trying . . . to eat . . . breakfast."

Uh-oh, Phoebe thought. *When Leo does that slow-talking thing, it's time to get out of the way. Suddenly,* Phoebe heard a sound that made her forget about Piper and Leo. *I think I hear the pitter-patter of Paige's mules on the stairs!*

Clunk-clunk-clunk-clunk.

Paige came into the dining room and flopped happily into a chair.

"I have two words for you," she said to Phoebe.

"They better not be 'ruined sweater,'" Phoebe quipped.

"Max Wolf."

"Good date?" Phoebe asked excitedly. "Tell all!"

"He's a dream!" Paige gushed. "It was so weird. My dates with all the other Kiss guys were so dull, I felt like I was walking through mud. But with Max it was like hiking in high altitude. Everything was crisp and clear. It was like my senses were heightened!"

"That sounds more like a marathon than a date," Phoebe joked, "but whatever rows your boat."

"Oh, it's hard to explain," Paige said. "All I know is, Max is it. I'm looking no further."

She popped out of her chair and went into the foyer to grab her purse. When she returned to the breakfast table, she was holding her Palm Pilot.

"Whoa," Phoebe said. "What are you doing?"

"Well, I've got a lot of dates to cancel, so I better get on it," Paige said, glancing at the end of the table where Leo and Piper were glaring at each other. "Leo, can you pass me the toast?"

When Leo ignored Paige, she glanced at Phoebe with her eyebrows raised.

"Married love," Phoebe whispered with a giggle. "It's a mystery."

"Not for long, it isn't," Cole said as he slipped into the dining room and gave Phoebe a kiss on the nape of her neck.

"Oh . . . hi, honey," Phoebe said with a

nervous laugh. "Paige was just about to do something crazy."

Paige looked up from her Palm Pilot in annoyance.

"Crazy? What crazy?" she protested. "Yesterday everyone was saying I was 'fast' for dating so many guys. Now I'm all ready to become a one-man woman and I'm nuts?"

"Honey, don't you think it's a little premature to commit to Max?" Piper chimed in, giving Leo a sidelong glance. "After all, it's amazing how long it takes to really get to know a person!"

"Hey!" Leo said. "What's that supposed to mean, Piper? You know, I think it's time for me to give you a little quiz. Let's see if you can take it as well as you can dish it out."

He reached across the table and snatched some of the papers stacked by Piper's elbow.

Phoebe rolled her eyes and returned her attention to Paige.

"Here's the thing," she said to her sister. "If you really think you want Max to be your boyfriend, the best thing you could do is keep dating other guys."

"And that makes sense, how?" Paige asked.

"Standard dating dogma," Phoebe said casually. "Love finds you only when you stop looking. The guy who likes you, you don't like. And the guy you like, doesn't like you. In other words, what you usually get in romance is the inverse of your desire."

"Uh-huh," Paige said, looking confused as Cole squinted at Phoebe in amusement.

"So you want Max all to yourself?" Phoebe concluded. "Show him how popular you are. Be a little unavailable. Desperation is sure to ensue."

"Phoebe," Cole joked, grabbing a slice of toast off her plate. "I had no idea you were such a player. What sort of wiles did you work on me when we first met?"

"No wiles for you, Cole," Phoebe said. "Just your standard falling in love, getting my heart broken, falling back in love and, hopefully, living happily ever after."

"Standard," Cole said, his eyes softening a bit. "Sure. But not for you. You were single-girl extraordinaire before we met."

Phoebe looked quickly at her plate. Her mind flashed on her former life—dating, dancing 'til dawn, each night on the town heightened by the possibility of meeting your soul mate. And the truth was, she'd never really expected to meet him, that mythical soul mate. Cole had jumped into her heart almost despite herself.

And now she was on the bridal fast track. It almost made her head spin.

Cole was staring at her, almost as if he could read her mind.

"I'm no Josh Skilling," he said, his voice low and rumbly. "Of course, maybe that's what you want."

"No . . ." Phoebe said. "'Course not."

"Are you sure about that?" Cole said. "Because I can see how being strung along by a guy with ice in his veins could be *really* appealing."

"Cole!" Phoebe looked up at him, feeling stung. Then she flounced out of her chair.

Phoebe glanced at Leo, who was flipping through Piper's quizzes and curling his lip.

Suddenly, I know just how Leo feels, being under the romantic microscope, Phoebe thought. *I think it's time to duck out from under the lens.*

"I'll get the dishes," she announced, grabbing her plate and avoiding Cole's eyes. She swung around to Paige's corner of the table and leaned in to pick up her sister's plate. As she did, her fingertips brushed Paige's turquoise Palm Pilot.

And that's when Phoebe felt the familiar rush.

She gasped and felt her head dive into some nebulous, shimmery place. Then her mind began to swim with frantic images. She was in full-on premonition mode.

She saw a young couple, embracing against a brick wall. The woman was blond and curvy. Her left hand was curled casually around her date's neck as he kissed her. Then, through the fog of the vision, Phoebe saw the girl's hand clench. She began to scratch at her suitor, struggling to get away.

Phoebe's mind flashed forward to the girl's body. Her chest was bathed in blood.

Next the scene replayed itself. The people were new, but the scenario was the same:

Kiss.

Kill.

Kiss.

Kill.

Phoebe was finally released from the premonition when the third girl fell, her pale hand landing in an oily puddle with a thud.

Phoebe gasped again and felt the breakfast plate she was holding fly from her hand, shattering at her feet. Clutching her temples in pain, she slumped to the floor and moaned.

"Phoebe!" Cole cried, jumping behind her to catch her head before it hit the floor. "What is it? What did you see?"

Phoebe gazed up at Cole and tried to forget the hostility that had been pulsing between them only a minute ago.

Because the young women in her vision had it a lot worse than her.

Their love had gotten them killed.

Chapter
4

Half an hour after Phoebe's premonition, Darryl Morris was at the front door. Piper had called him immediately.

"Hey, guys," Darryl said, stepping into the foyer and giving Piper and her sisters a warm smile. Piper handed him a cup of coffee and patted his shoulder.

What would we do without Darryl? she thought with a sigh. *Sometimes I can't believe how lucky we were to become friends with a police detective who lets us collaborate on cases* and *isn't freaked by our supernatural selves. We've never had to worry about Darryl blowing our cover.*

"So does Phoebe's premonition mean anything to you?" Piper asked, guiding Darryl into the conservatory. The rest of the group was camped out in the sun-filled room, lounging on the pretty white wicker furniture.

Phoebe still looked a little pale and shaky. Her premonitions always seemed to drain her of energy. It was the most debilitating of any of the sisters' powers, which sometimes made Piper feel guilty. She sat on the arm of Phoebe's chair and put a protective arm around her shoulders as Darryl started talking.

"I was literally reaching for the phone to call you when you rang me up, Piper," he said, settling his big, bearish frame onto one of the loveseats. "There were three murders last night— all very similar. And definitely supernatural."

"How can you tell?" Paige said in alarm. "What happened to them?"

"Well, the bodies are still in the pathology lab, but initial reports say there were no weapons used," Darryl said.

"But in my premonition," Phoebe said, "there was so much blood!"

"And your mind didn't lie," Darryl said grimly. "These girls' hearts had been ripped from their chests. And I don't know any human who would be capable of sucking a heart out of a chest cavity without so much as a penknife."

Piper flinched at the image.

These are the moments I most loathe our witchy lifestyle, she thought. *Who else has to deal with death and demons on, like, a weekly basis?*

She stood up wearily and said, "So, girls, the usual? Book of Shadows? Scrying for demon locations?"

"You got it," Phoebe said.

"I guess I better call and cancel my brunch date," Paige said.

"Actually, maybe that's not such a good idea," Leo piped up. He was standing behind Paige with that thoughtful look he always got when he was in Whitelighter mode. "Phoebe, you got your premonition after touching Paige's Palm Pilot, right?"

"Uh-huh," Phoebe said. "At least I think that's what set it off."

"So . . . maybe whatever's in the Palm Pilot could lead us to the demon," Leo said.

"What?!" Paige said shakily. "But my whole life is in there! Addresses for everyone I know. A calendar for the past year. I don't know how we'd get through it all."

"Okay, the Palm Pilot isn't the best clue," Piper said. "But the victims might be. Darryl, do you know anything about them?"

"Well, they all fit the same profile—midtwenties, attractive, single. Names are . . ."

Darryl flipped through a file, then read, "Christy Farthington, Betsy Pollack, Carla Janowski."

"Ahhh!" Phoebe cried. "Carla Janowski? I know her! I saw her just a few days ago!"

"You're kidding," Piper said. "Oh, honey, I'm sorry. Was she a close friend? I've never heard you mention her."

Phoebe slumped back into her wicker chair with tears in her eyes.

"No, we just had some classes together at school," she said, her voice trembling with guilt. "In fact, I didn't even like her that much. But Carla was harmless. I can't believe she's been murdered."

Darryl sat down on the edge of the coffee table and leaned toward Phoebe.

"Phoebe, think. Did Carla say anything to you that might help us?" he urged.

Phoebe shook her head and shrugged.

"I don't know," she said. "She was all excited about my engagement, I remember. And she was bumming out about being single."

Suddenly Phoebe gasped and stared at Paige.

"Carla was the one who told me about Kiss.com," she breathed. "She'd just signed up for the service."

"Now, *that's* a clue," Leo said. Then he turned to Paige. "Which means you better not be late for your date."

"Are you kidding?" Paige squealed, jumping off the couch. "What if this serial killer is my brunch date? What then?"

"Then I orb you out of there," Leo said. "What, did you think I'd let you go alone?"

Piper saw Paige relax a little bit. But *just* a little bit.

"Look, Paige," she said. "The odds that your date is our demon are slim. I mean, none of your other Kissers tried to steal your heart, right?"

"Not lethally, anyway," Cole said with a slight smile.

"I guess you're right," Paige said. "And with Leo with me, it'll probably be just fine."

"Totally," Phoebe said, jumping off the chair. She'd recovered from her shock.

When Phoebe gets gung ho, Piper thought with a smile, *stand back*.

"Okay, so we have a plan," Phoebe announced. "Paige and Leo will go scan Mr. Coffee Date for horns and scales. And while you're gone, Piper and I will do our Book of Shadows thing."

"You make it almost sound fun," Paige said, hauling herself to her feet. She slumped into the foyer and grabbed her purse.

"Let me tell you, Paige," Phoebe said, "after a few years of the Wiccan life, you get used to it."

"Sad but true," Piper said. "All right, guys. Let's get to work."

Ninety minutes later, everyone's enthusiasm had definitely cooled.

"Okay, is our crystal on the blink?" Phoebe complained. She was in the attic of Halliwell Manor with Piper, scrying. That is, she was dangling a magic crystal over a map of San Francisco. The crystal was supposed to drop when it hit the place where a demon was lurking.

But today the crystal was not cooperating.

She'd checked everywhere, even in the far reaches of the 'burbs. But their demon seemed to be AWOL.

"I don't get it," Piper said from her perch behind the lectern where they kept the Book of Shadows. "This demon's holding three human hearts. And he's also got time to disappear into thin air?"

She went back to flipping through the Book. If anybody had a jaundiced eye about being a witch, it was Piper. But when she was studying the Book of Shadows she couldn't help but feel awe. After all, generations of Halliwell women had created this book with its supple, leather cover and age-yellowed, parchment pages. Over the centuries they'd written about demons, warlocks, and other random evils they'd come across.

But over the years Piper and her sisters had also learned—the hard way—that the Book of Shadows didn't have all the answers.

And this was clearly one of those times. She'd flipped through much of the Book, but hadn't spotted any demon that stole hearts.

"Well, I guess we can be thankful for one thing," Phoebe said, as she let the crystal hover above a street corner on the map. "I'm at the restaurant where Paige is having brunch and there's no demon there."

"There's no Paige there either," Paige said as she appeared at the attic door. There were shadows beneath her eyes and she was totally devoid of post-date pep. Leo slumped up the stairs behind Paige.

"What happened?" Phoebe cried, dropping the crystal on the map and running to the attic door. "You both look like you've been through the wringer."

"Only the most boring date ever," Paige yawned. "The veterinarian was no demon. I would have welcomed the *diversion* of a demon. On the plus side, I have coupons for all of us. Free spaying or neutering for all our pets."

"Don't listen to her, Sweetie," Phoebe said. She reached down to cover the ears of the sisters' Siamese cat, who'd been lurking around her feet as she scryed. Every witch had a familiar and Sweetie was theirs. "We'll get some kittens out of you yet."

Leo stole over to Piper with a pained look on his face.

"And you think *I* need a relationship quiz?" he hissed. "You should have seen the two of them. I could hear the sighs of boredom all the way over at my table ten feet away. It's like they had nothing to say."

Piper gave him a look and put her finger to her lips. Then she walked over to Paige and gave her a sympathetic frown.

"Well, you did one for the home team, Paige," she said. "At least we know he's not a demon!"

"Arrrrgggh," Paige said, yawning loudly as she gave Piper a lame nod. "I'm hungry. Is there anything to eat downstairs."

"Hello," Leo gasped, "didn't I just see you eat an entire spinach frittata with a side of hash browns?"

"I know," Paige said with a shrug. "But somehow I feel so empty. It's like that date drained me of something."

Paige headed to the stairs with Piper, Phoebe and Leo on her heels.

"Not to add to the gloom, but I do feel I should point out that we're still demonless," Piper said as the group headed to the kitchen. "If we have to screen Paige's suitors date-by-date, I'm afraid we're going to lose more innocents in the meantime."

"She's right," Phoebe said, biting her lip. She flopped into the desk chair and fiddled with the computer's mouse. "We need to broaden our reach. Go somewhere that's crawling with men on the make."

"And come to think of it, I have to go to work tonight," Piper said, winking at her sister. "At a nightclub that happens to be crawling with men on the make."

"P3," Leo said. "Perfect. Paige will be bait."

Paige, who'd been rifling through the fridge in search of munchies, groaned. She emerged with an apple and a glare.

"Me? Again?" she sputtered. "Why not Piper or Phoebe?"

"Paige, we own P3," Piper said. "Everyone knows Phoebe and I aren't single."

"How convenient," Paige grumbled. Then she grabbed a jar of peanut butter from the pantry, smeared a big gob of the stuff onto her apple, and took a big, irritable bite.

"Ugh, why did you let me eat so much this afternoon?" Paige groaned. It was 11 P.M. that night, prime pick-up hour at P3. And unlike most Saturday nights of her life, Paige couldn't have been less in the mood. She was slumped over the bar, in a post-binge haze.

"Don't worry, you look great. I particularly like the electric blue, rubber dress, Paige," Piper said as she wiped off glasses behind the bar. She peeked over the bar and grinned. "And four-inch heels. Really completes the package."

"Listen, I only want to have to be bait once," Paige said, taking a loud slurp of her diet soda. "I'm going to make it count. And I'm going to snare us a demon."

"That's the spirit," Cole said as he and Phoebe bellied up to the bar. "Paige, you look positively . . . fetching."

"Thanks for the diplomacy," Paige said. She knew she looked outrageous, even for her. She opened her tiny blue purse and pulled out a compact to swipe another smear of hot-pink gloss onto her lips.

"Well, I better go play fetch," she said. Giving her sisters a tremulous wave and glancing at Leo, who was stationed near the club door, she plunged into the throng.

Funny how flirting, dancing, and picking up dudes becomes a total chore once you have to do it, Paige thought, giving a guy on the dance floor an exaggerated wink as she sidled up next to him.

Ugh, smell that cologne, she complained to herself as she began shimmying her hips and smiling at the circle of men that quickly formed around her.

"Hi, what's your name?" she cooed to one with a particularly prominent—possibly demonic?—forehead.

"All you need to know about me, baby, is this," said the guy. Then he reached into his pocket.

Paige felt her heart leap.

Is he reaching for a weapon? she thought as her breath started coming in shallow gasps. She spun around to look for Leo or her sisters. But she couldn't see a thing except a whole lot of leering, dancing men.

Jingle, jingle, jingle.

Fearfully Paige turned back to Mr. Forehead. He was thrusting something at her; a key chain.

"That's right. I drive a Lexus, sweetheart," he said. "Want to see it?"

Okay, he's asking me to step outside, Paige thought. *Maybe he's our guy. Although, could a demon possibly be this cheesy?*

Reluctantly Paige forced a sultry smile and put her hand in Mr. Forehead's sweaty one.

"All right," she agreed. Then she followed him toward P3's door. Trailing behind him, she hopped up and down and waved to attract her sisters' attention. Piper spotted her and motioned Phoebe and Cole toward the door.

As they climbed the stairs to P3's door, Paige cringed at the clamminess of Mr. Forehead's hand.

Is it because he's a demon or just a loser? she wondered, feeling her heart pound beneath her rubber dress.

Mr. Forehead pulled her through the door. Paige glanced behind her. Leo and the rest of their group were on their way. But just as the door swung shut, Mr. Forehead wrenched his hand from hers.

She spun to look at him, feeling a rush of panic make her face go hot. But instead of confronting a demon with his eye on her thoracic region, she saw . . . Josh Skilling? It was! Josh Skilling, her very first, and very lamest, Kiss.com date. Not to mention, Phoebe's ex.

And here was the weird part. Josh had gone all commando on her. He'd been the one who'd ripped Mr. Forehead away from her side. Now he was tossing the hapless player across P3's parking lot with more strength than a skinny guy like him should have possessed.

"Josh?" Paige gasped. "What are you doing here?"

"Rescuing you, that's what," Josh said, staring at Paige with fiery eyes. Before she could make a sound, he grabbed her arm. Then he whisked her toward the corner of the building. Paige tried to wrench away from him, but his fingers dug into her flesh like talons. Paige glanced over her shoulder just before Josh pulled her around the corner. The club door was just beginning to inch open. Which meant her sisters hadn't seen a thing. And now, they wouldn't be able to see her, either!

Paige opened her mouth, ready to unleash the loudest scream she could muster. But Josh clamped his hand over her mouth.

"What's wrong, Paige?" Josh said. Then his face split into an incredulous smile.

"Wait a minute," he said. "Don't tell me you're scared of me? Sid . . . *he* is the guy you should be screaming about."

Paige batted Josh's hand away from her face. Luckily he unwrapped his fingers from her arm, too. Paige wondered if he'd left a bruise.

"Sid?" Paige breathed. She peered at Josh in confusion. He knew Mr. Forehead by name? "You know him?"

"That guy is such trouble," Josh said. "Not a

gentleman at all, let me tell you. I'm surprised you haven't caught wind of his reputation."

"Been too busy . . . on the Internet, I guess," Paige said weakly.

"And I'm glad of that," Josh said. "You know Paige, I really liked you when we went out the other night."

"You did?" Paige said. Josh was acting almost normal now. He even seemed a little sweet.

But as she peered into his eyes, she realized— something was off. His stare was too intense. Too focused. Despite his warm words, his voice was remote. The natural friendliness of the other night had disappeared.

"I did, Paige," Josh said. "In fact, I'm glad I ran into you. And not so I could rescue you from that skank, Sid."

"Why else?" Paige said apprehensively. She leaned back against the clammy brick wall of P3's alley. Her eyes shifted away from Josh's just for an instant. She was really, really hoping to see Phoebe, Piper, or the guys emerging from the darkness. But they were nowhere to be seen.

"Because," Josh said, leaning in. His voice got deeper, almost robotic. And his face began to change too, darkening into a sinister glower. Paige could feel his breath—hot and fetid—gust onto her face. "You've got my heart."

Paige glanced down and saw Josh's hand, reaching toward her chest. His arm was shaking, as if infused with some sort of electricity. And as his fingertips brushed the bare skin above the low-cut bodice of her dress, his nails instantly grew into glinting talons. In fact, his entire hand transformed into a metallic, clawlike, lethal weapon.

Paige recoiled, pressing herself back into the wall. Her mouth flew open and she tried to scream. But she felt as if her lungs had collapsed. She had no air to breathe, much less scream.

Paige felt one, silvery nail pierce her skin. Heat shot into her chest with a searing rush and a rivulet of blood spilled onto her skin.

And at last pain broke Paige's silence.

"AAAAIIIGGGH!" she shrieked, trying to squirm away from Josh's mutated, menacing hand. She grabbed his robotic wrist and tried to push it away, but he was like a pillar of stone. He wasn't budging.

Instead he pressed on, gouging another knife-like claw into her chest. Paige screamed again, then choked out a terrified sob.

"Pipeeeeeeer!" she yelled. "Phooooeeeee—"

"Hi-yah!"

Before Paige even saw her coming, Phoebe's foot connected with Josh's head. He crashed to the ground, leaving a long gash on Paige's arm as he fell.

Phoebe had launched into him with such a powerful roundhouse kick that her feet flew out from under her as well. She landed on top of Josh with a painful thud.

"He's the demon!" Paige screamed. "Watch out!"

Phoebe quickly rolled off of Josh, then pushed herself into a reverse handspring. She landed on her feet, in full kung-fu fighting stance. At the same time, Josh stumbled to his feet too. He lashed out at Phoebe with his talons, but she ducked the strike easily.

Then Paige saw Phoebe's eyes travel to Josh's face. She blanched. Her fists fell to her sides and her mouth popped open.

"Josh?" she squeaked.

"Josh?" Cole bellowed. "Josh, the 'friend'? This guy is suddenly everywhere you go!"

"And he's also a demon!" Piper said, stepping forward with gritted teeth. She raised her arms and reared back. Paige knew what was coming next. With one flick of her fingers, Piper was going to blow Josh to smithereens. The first time Paige had seen Piper do this, she'd completely freaked. *I mean, who else has a big sister who'd make you tea and cookies one moment, then explode villains the next?*

Not that Paige was complaining now.

She squeezed her eyes shut and braced herself for the boom.

But what she heard instead was Phoebe, calling out, "No! Wait!"

Paige's eyes flew open as she saw Piper hesitate and glare at Phoebe.

"What the—" Piper said.

And that was the only window Josh needed. While Piper stared at her sister, the demon spun on his heel and fled. Within seconds he'd ducked into a shadow and rounded a corner. Piper took off after him, pounding the pavement impressively in her high heels and leather pants. But as she hit the end of the alley and turned to the right, her shoulders slumped.

Josh had gotten away.

Piper turned and stalked back down the alley, glaring at her sister.

"'No, wait?'" she spat through gritted teeth. "You just cost us our demon, Phoebe. And you may have cost another innocent her life!"

Chapter

5

Phoebe watched her sister stalk down the alley, glaring at her with venom. Phoebe hadn't seen Piper this mad since she used Piper's favorite whisk to highlight her hair.

"What were you thinking?!" Piper demanded, coming to a halt in front of Phoebe and crossing her arms over her chest.

"Yeah, he was our guy," Paige said. "And I've got the bloody welts to prove it. Um, Leo, could I get some healing over here?"

Phoebe felt tears well up in her eyes as she looked at her little sister's super-pale skin. Two horrible-looking puncture wounds in her chest were oozing blood, and a gash on her bicep looked raw and ugly. Leo ran up to Paige and placed his hands on her wounds. A white glow emanated from his palms and in a moment, the blood melted away. Paige's skin was flawless once again.

Which could *not* be said for Phoebe's relationship with Cole. Not after she'd just saved the life
of her sorry ex. If Cole had been angry with
Phoebe, she could have handled it. But by the
clench in his jaw and the hooded look that shad-
owed his blue eyes, she could tell he was worse
than mad. He was hurt. And confused.

"Phoebe," he said in a low, stiff voice. "Do
you want to explain to me what just happened?"

"I do," Phoebe said. Then her voice stopped
in her throat. She bit her lip, and started to talk.
Then she paused again and put her finger to her
chin.

"Okay, here's the thing," she finally choked
out. "I stopped Piper because . . ."

Phoebe trailed off and stared helplessly at her
family. Why *had* she saved Josh Skilling—a.k.a.,
heartsucking demon from hell—from being van-
quished? She didn't like him. She didn't even
know him anymore! And, she had to face it,
she'd had boyfriends turn into demons in the
past. She'd had no problem turning them into
little poofs of smoke.

So why had she made an exception for Josh?

"I guess I just . . . you know, blast from the
past and all," Phoebe yammered. "It just caught
me off guard."

"Uh-huh," Cole said. "Okay, Phoebe. Whatever
you say."

"Cole . . ." Phoebe began, but then she
stopped herself. What could she say? The deed

was done. And she didn't even know what it meant, other than . . . maybe she really *wasn't* bride material! She watched Cole wander away, knowing that his perfect posture and squared shoulders were only masking his hurt pride.

Sighing, Phoebe turned back to her sisters. Paige was skimming her fingers over her phantom wounds. Then she shook her head in confusion.

"Wait a minute," she sputtered. "I'm just finding it a little hard to believe that Josh Skilling, thirty-year-old software designer and Kiss.com subscriber, is also a demon!"

"It's always hard to believe, honey," Piper said, giving Cole a quick glance. Luckily he was out of earshot. "We've all swapped spit with demons along the way."

"Ex-*cuse* me, but I did not swap spit with Josh Skilling!" Paige protested.

This time it was *Phoebe* Piper was eyeballing. Phoebe rolled her eyes and said, "Okay, can we stop with the discussing of Josh Skilling's bodily fluids and move on to his manicure? Those were some pretty killer claws!"

"Yeah, definitely demonic, I'd say," Piper said.

"Well, there's one way to find out for sure," Phoebe said. "We have to find Josh."

"Naturally," Cole interjected sarcastically. Phoebe looked up in surprise. Cole had rejoined the group, but he was clearly still seething.

"Cole," Phoebe said, "I'm sorry I made that stupid mistake. And we definitely need to talk about it. But right now innocents are at stake."

"I know," Cole said, and Phoebe was sure she saw his eyes soften, just a little. "Go. I'll be back at the Manor if you need me."

"I do, you know," Phoebe said tremulously. "Need you."

Cole looked at his feet quickly. Then he nodded brusquely and walked away.

"Why don't you go with him?" Piper said to Leo. "You go have some guy time. The Power of Three can take it from here."

"All right," Leo said, giving Piper a quick peck and glancing at Phoebe. "Maybe I'll, uh, give one of those relationship quizzes another chance."

"Hel-lo," Phoebe blurted. "I can hear you! It was just a stupid mistake. It doesn't mean Cole and I are in trouble."

"Uh, we better hit it," Piper said, widening her eyes at Leo. "Be ready to orb in if we need you, okay?"

"You got it," Leo said, before turning to trot after Cole.

Phoebe and her sisters headed for the SUV.

"Well, where should we look for demonic Josh?" Paige said. "Is there some after hours club for boogeymen in this burg?"

"Paige, we live in San Francisco," Piper said. "There are no demon bars. My guess is Josh has probably gotten himself off the streets."

Then she gave Phoebe a meaningful look.

"All right, all right, I do know where his apartment is," Phoebe said, rolling her eyes.

Paige stifled a laugh as she crawled into the backseat.

"Ah-ah-ah," Phoebe said, turning to glare at her from the front seat. "Need I bring up your last beau, Lung Chow? We've all made some less-than-savvy dating choices, haven't we?"

"Touché," Paige said, though her lips were still quivering with laughter.

"Piper," Phoebe said, turning around to glare through the windshield. "Just drive. I'll tell you where to go."

Fifteen minutes later the Halliwells were parked on the street outside a funky old apartment building. Phoebe peered out the window and saw a light on in Josh's apartment, a second floor studio around the back.

"Well, if he does indeed still live here," Phoebe said, "it looks like he's home."

"And there's a back stairwell," Piper noted as she followed Phoebe's gaze. "Perfect. Let's move."

The sisters tiptoed down a walkway beside the building, then slowly climbed the ramshackled wooden fire escape to Josh's door. When they reached the landing, Phoebe peeked inside.

"I see him," she whispered. She was looking into a brightly lit kitchen. Directly beyond the kitchen, through a large, open doorway, was the living room. The lights were off in the living room, but in the shadows Phoebe could just make out Josh. She couldn't tell what he was doing—all she could see was his back.

Then Phoebe caught her breath. She saw a flash of silver glint in the light of the kitchen. Then she heard a muffled scream.

"It looks like Josh has found some other company for the evening," Piper cried.

"Stand back," Phoebe barked at her sisters. Then she balled her fists beneath her chin, spun around quickly, and used the momentum to slam her foot into Josh's kitchen door. She felt the door splinter beneath her heel with a satisfying cracking noise.

Piper thrust her hands through the rough hole in the door and flicked her fingers.

Instantly Josh and his terrified prey froze. All sounds that might have been rattling around the apartment—the humming of the refrigerator, the drip of a leaky faucet, or the hiss of a radiator—halted as well. The witches plunged into the eerily quiet apartment.

Paige looked frantically around the spare apartment for something that could be used to fight off the demon. But it was a total bachelor pad with nothing but a cheap dinette set, a foam-stuffed couch, mini-blinds on the windows, not even a dishtowel hanging on the refrigerator door.

Then she glanced down at the leather trench coat she'd thrown over her slinky dress in the car. She ripped off its belt and tossed it triumphantly to Phoebe. Phoebe and Piper positioned themselves on either side of Josh, ready to grab his hands. And Paige wrapped her arms around Josh's "date"—a beautiful woman who couldn't have been more than twenty-one. Her blue eyes were horrified—bulging and watery.

They were ready.

Paige nodded at Piper, who used another flick of her fingers to unfreeze Josh and the girl. The minute Josh started moving, Phoebe and Piper pounced on him. Phoebe grabbed the hand with the glinting claws and wrenched it behind his back, yanking his shoulder joint painfully.

Meanwhile Paige pulled the innocent away from Josh with an awkward jerking motion that sent both of them tumbling to the floor. The girl looked at the bizarre scene that had unfolded while she was frozen and burst into tearful screams.

"You're okay," Paige told her. "You just need to get out of here. Now!"

The girl didn't need to be told twice. She stumbled to her feet and bolted through the splintered door.

While the innocent's footsteps echoed down the back stairs, Piper and Phoebe pulled Josh into the kitchen, shoved him into a straight-back chair, and wrapped Paige's belt around his chest. In two shakes he was bound, but not—unfortunately—gagged.

"Unleash me," Josh sputtered, glaring at Phoebe. "You'll be sorry, should you not. Sorrier even than the rest of them."

"What are you talking about, Josh?" Phoebe spat, leaning into Josh's face. "I want an explanation. That was my *sister* you were trying to murder back there at P3."

"Your sister?" Josh spat back. "Who are you?"

Phoebe pulled back in shock. Was it possible that Josh didn't recognize her?

Something isn't right, here, Phoebe thought. *Either that or Josh the Demon is trying to psyche me out. Well it isn't going to work. Not a second time around.*

"Maybe this will remind you who I am, Josh," she said. Then she reared back and threw a punch that connected neatly with Josh's cheekbone. The strength she'd built up during all her workouts with Cole really paid off. Josh's head whipped to the side like a pinwheel.

"Uh-oh," Paige said as Josh's head wobbled for a moment, then sagged limply. "I don't think we're going to get any explanation out of Josh now. You knocked him out cold, Phoebe. You kung-fu queen."

"And that will make it all the easier to vanquish his cowardly butt," Piper announced. She reared back, ready to blow Josh up. But before she could make the lethal motion, a gooey substance began oozing out of his ear.

"Okay, what's that?" Piper asked, her hands still poised next to her ears.

Phoebe stared at the silvery, gelatinous goo dripping down the side of Josh's face. It wasn't gray matter—even *she* couldn't have done that kind of damage with one punch. And it certainly wasn't blood.

As the sisters stared, the silvery trickle turned into a gush. It spilled off Josh's shoulder but before it hit the kitchen linoleum, the rivulet veered upward. It shot into the middle of the room. Then the silver gush began to expand.

"This is definitely not what I expected," Paige said, staring in fascination as the goo began to elongate and hollow out. It continued to grow until it became a giant tube of some sort. At the end of the tube, a giant mouth began to take shape, complete with rubbery, mushy lips.

And then, as if the tube had unleashed a giant sneeze, the sisters were buffeted by a hot blast of air.

"I guess this is some sort of demonic weapon," Phoebe called over the loud rush of wind.

The surge of air didn't stop. In fact it grew stronger every second, speeding up and spinning around itself like a tiny tornado. All the while the wind made a horrendous, screeching howl.

"What are you waiting for?" Paige screamed to Piper, her hair whipping around her cheeks. "Zap him before that . . . thing gets any bigger!"

"But we don't know what that *thing* is!" Piper yelled back. "All we know is that this demon spewed it out. Kill the demon and we might be stuck with something even worse."

"When did you get so logical?" Phoebe shrieked at Piper.

"When I became the oldest Charmed One," Piper yelled back, locking sad, panicked eyes with Phoebe for a brief instant. Then they turned back to the silvery blob taking shape before them.

And its shape was clearly that of a long, blustery tunnel now. Its opening, hovering above the floor and pulsating, was about six feet in diameter. The interior of the tunnel, which seemed to extend *way* beyond Josh's little kitchen, was lined with gushy, silvery stuff.

"Is it animal or mineral, do you think?" Piper called.

"It looks way too carnivorous to be vegetable," Paige shrieked. She grabbed Piper's arm and clung to her in terror.

And that's when Josh woke up.

He shook his head blearily, then slowly lifted his eyes to look around. After gaping for a stunned moment at the esophaguslike *thing* that had taken over his little apartment, he blinked hard and stared at the sisters.

"Paige?" he called. "What are you doing he—Phoebe?! Oh my God. Phoebe . . . what's . . . what's happening?"

"You're telling me you don't know?" Phoebe yelled, planting her feet angrily on the floor. The wind seemed to be whipping around her harder. Her hair was fluttering over her eyes, half-blinding her. She had to scream to be heard.

"You caused all this!" she continued. "You with your big, stupid claw-hand and oozy ear!"

"What?" Josh yelled back. "What are you talking about? And how did you get here? And . . . and what *is* that thing?! Phoebe, untie me. Please!"

Phoebe looked back at her sisters, who were fighting off the wind too busy to pay attention. Josh seemed so different now. Or rather he seemed the same. This was the Josh she'd known. The voice, the face—he was familiar again.

Or maybe he was conning her.

The decision was hers. Remembering Piper's rage in the alley, not to mention Cole's confusion, Phoebe shook her head. She was going to do the right thing.

"No," she announced to Josh. She held her hand in front of her eyes, which were stinging from the searing wind. "You're a demon. I won't be duped."

"Demon?" Josh screamed. "Phoebe, I know our relationship didn't end well, but this is extreme!"

"I—I don't know . . ." Phoebe began. But she was interrupted by a harsh, scraping sound.

"Aaaaarggh!" Josh screamed. His chair had just lurched three feet across the hardwood floor. Three feet closer to the tunnel. He was being drawn inside.

"Phoebe, get away!" Piper yelled.

Phoebe nodded vaguely, stepping back a bit. But as Josh's chair was jerked sideways again, her hand flew to her mouth. The chair tipped over and Josh crashed to the floor. He struggled madly to free himself of the leather belt, but Piper's knots were too tight. He was trapped.

"This is cra—Phoebe! Paige? *Somebody.* Please!" Josh screamed. "Help me!"

Without another word, Phoebe leapt over to Josh.

"Phoebe, what're you doing?" Piper yelled.

"It's him," Phoebe called back to her. "The old Josh."

Josh's chair was being dragged continuously across the floor. He was struggling so hard, his head was hitting the floor with pathetic thunks.

Phoebe lunged for him, wrapping her arms around his chest from behind. The back of the chair dug painfully into her ribs, but she hung on and braced herself.

"Noooo!" she heard Paige shout. Then

Paige's voice was cut off by the tornado of wind. Phoebe's feet scrabbled on the floor as she pulled back on Josh's body.

But he continued to inch toward the mouth of the tunnel.

And he was dragging Phoebe with him.

Threading one arm through the slats of Josh's chair back, she twisted around to see Piper and Paige teetering on the edge of what looked like a whirlpool of wind. Phoebe realized now what she'd done. She'd jumped across a divide. Whatever was outside of the tornado—which was now bristling with stuff from Josh's apartment, from books to a lamp to a small ottoman— was safe. And whatever was trapped inside, was going down the tunnel.

Namely Phoebe and Josh.

Piper was waving her hands frantically, but clearly her magic was useless against this demonic vacuum cleaner. So she reached into the whirl, trying to grab Phoebe.

Phoebe waved her away.

"Stay back!" she screamed. "Don't get sucked in!"

And then Piper disappeared from view. As did Paige and the rest of Josh's apartment.

The mouth of the tunnel had gobbled them up.

The next thing Phoebe knew, she and Josh were tumbling through the tunnel at an insane speed. Phoebe, screaming, felt the skin on her face tighten as they plunged into a silvery, mushy, seemingly endless abyss. As Phoebe clung desperately to Josh, who might have been yelling even louder than she was, her mind flashed on the last words she'd screamed to her sister.

"Don't get sucked in!" she'd ordered her.

See, that's the problem with me, she thought as panicked tears began streaming from her eyes. *I never follow my own advice.*

Phoebe had no idea how long she and Josh had been in freefall. Actually it wasn't a total freefall. The walls of the tunnel had seemed to close in on them, encasing them in slippery, soft, sucking stuff. It literally felt like they were being squeezed and swallowed through an enormous esophagus.

"Please let us not be the afternoon snack of some enormous, meat-eating creature," Phoebe whispered. She gazed up at Josh. He was about fifteen feet above her. Finally he'd untangled himself from the chair. The force of the fall must have untied the knots. He too had stopped screaming and seemed to be in shock. His limbs hung limply, defeated.

Since she had nothing else to do as her body hurtled through the abyss, Phoebe repeated her little prayer.

Please let me not be plummeting into the acid-filled stomach of some space creature, she thought.

*Or into some underworld pool of fire. Or some other
dimension where everybody has pointy ears or two
heads. Let it be a slow road to China. Or some supernatural amusement park. Or even a portal to
another—*

"Argh!" she screamed as she felt her butt hit
something hard.

Then she shrieked again as she saw *Josh's* butt
coming right at her head. She rolled out of the
way just before he made his own awkward crash
landing.

Phoebe laid on her stomach for a moment,
breathing hard, her face pressed into the
unyielding surface on which she'd landed. She
could see Josh, flopped out next to her. And she
could see that the hard surface seemed to be
made of stone tiles.

Stone, Phoebe thought. *That's an earthly substance. That's a good start.*

Painfully, she lifted her head off the floor and
lurched to her hands and knees. She coughed
raspily as she brushed silvery gook from her
clothes.

*I had to wear my favorite suede pants and a halter
top to P3*, she thought irritably. So *not a practical
travel outfit.*

She lurched to her feet and Josh did the same.

"Where are we?" he said, looking around
wildly. Phoebe followed his gaze. They'd landed
in a small chamber, constructed of the same,
sand-colored stone that lined the floor.

Phoebe pointed to a wall opposite them. It was flanked by openings, hung with rough curtains, instead of doors. And on the wall was a mural. It was straight out of a natural history museum's ancient Egypt exhibition. The figures in the mural, who all seemed to be bowing to a king, wore long bound beards and striped head-dresses.

There was just one thing that jarred Phoebe.

This was no ancient, dusty relic. This painting was fresh and very recent-looking.

Phoebe looked around at the rough sand-stone architecture, the homespun curtains, and the stone benches. And then she hung her head.

"Not again," she sighed.

"Not again, what?" Josh said. "What, Phoebe? Where the hell are we? Have you been here before?"

"Not here," she said. "But I've been to Massachusetts in the 1600s and San Francisco in the 1920s. I've been possessed by an antique mobster's moll. I know the signs."

"The signs of what?" Josh demanded. "Phoebe, you're making no sense."

"The signs of time travel," she said matter-of-factly. "But on the bright side, we haven't landed in some supernatural digestive system."

Josh seemed less-than-comforted. He was gazing at Phoebe, looking utterly lost. Instinctively they both looked at the ceiling.

The silvery maw that had just deposited them

into this place had disappeared. All they saw now was a low, primitive stone ceiling.

"This is *not* good," Josh said in a trembly voice.

"Finally, Josh," Phoebe breathed, trying to stop her hands from shaking, "we agree on something."

Chapter
6

"Noooo!" Paige was screaming. Through a blur of tears, she watched Phoebe and Josh slide toward the mouth of the bizarre, mouthlike tunnel that had, somehow, sprung from Josh's left ear.

Paige saw Phoebe glance over her shoulder and lock eyes with Piper. She knew Phoebe and Piper both lived in constant fear of losing another sister. And traveling between them, in that one instantaneous look, Paige knew was a wealth of communication—*Don't go. I'm sorry. Good-bye.*

Piper lurched forward, but Paige grabbed her shoulders and yanked her away from the swirl of air howling around the tunnel's mouth.

"You'll only get sucked in!" she screamed.

Phoebe, too, waved Piper away and called out to her. But her words were drowned by the howling of the wind.

The chair to which Josh was bound scraped across the hardwood floor, leaving splintery gashes in the boards. But for some reason, Phoebe hung on.

And when Josh, chair and all, was sucked into the pulsating, throatlike tunnel, Phoebe went with him.

In a blink they disappeared from view. Immediately afterward the tunnel's pulsating opening began to crumple in on itself. The mouth got smaller and smaller, until it closed completely. Then with a last, loud *whoosh* of air, the tunnel itself contracted until it simply poofed away.

Piper fell to her knees as Paige spun around in confusion. Josh's apartment was destroyed. Broken plates and shredded books littered the floor. Several windows had shattered. A lamp was crushed and lying on its side. The pillows had all been sucked from the living room couch.

And the worst part was the silence. A cold, eerie, perfectly still silence. Paige almost wondered if sound would emerge when she opened her mouth.

"What . . . just . . . happened?" she croaked.

"The usual," Piper said, stifling a sob. "Some horrible, supernatural force has stolen one of the Charmed Ones. And now we have to get her back."

Piper lurched to her feet and stalked through the kitchen toward the splintered back door. She batted at a chair that blocked her path and sent it skidding across the room. Then, with Paige at her heels, she stomped down the stairs and ran to their SUV. The women jumped into the car and Paige barely had time to close the passenger door before Piper skidded out into the street.

The quickest route home was through one of the city's most hopping bar strips. But Piper had forgotten it was Saturday night. The street was clogged with college kids cruising slowly in their sports cars and Jeeps. Pretty soon Piper and Paige's car was stuck in standstill traffic.

"Dammit," Piper said, glaring at the car in front of them. It was bouncing to the beat of some bass-heavy hip hop. "We don't have time for this!"

Paige bit her lip and felt another wave of panicky tears clog her throat. She gazed helplessly at the side of the street, listlessly scanning the throngs of scantily clad clubbers who were stalking down the sidewalk or waiting in line to get into some trendy new spot.

Then she gave a start.

"I know that guy," she said, pointing to a slim young man with auburn hair. "That's Stuart. I went out with him yesterday. He's from Kiss.com."

"And? . . ." Piper said. She was still glaring at the cars in front of her.

"And he's with a girl," Paige said, following Stuart with her eyes. He was walking with his arm through that of a pretty young woman. They were cruising pretty quickly down the sidewalk.

"Paige," Piper said, "isn't it a little early to get jealous. You had one date with the guy."

"I'm so not jealous," Paige said, squinting at Stuart and the woman. "I mean, Stuart was not exactly hunky. Unless you like that skinny, short, bespectacled Woody Allen type. What I am is . . . suspicious. Does it look to you like that girl wants to be dragged down the street that way?"

"What?" Piper said. She leaned over Paige's lap to peer out the car window. They both stared for a moment as Stuart's hand tightened around the girl's upper arm. She gave him a sidelong look that was part irritation and part fear.

And then, abruptly, Stuart ducked into an alley, roughly jerking the woman around the corner.

"I think we should check this out," Paige said, gnawing her lip.

"We don't have time!" Piper protested. "We have to focus on Phoebe."

"We're stuck in traffic anyway," Paige countered. "And think about it, Piper, there was more than one woman killed. Maybe there's more than one heartsucker! Maybe Josh wasn't the only one."

Piper stared dubiously at the mouth of the dark alley for a moment. Then without another word she jumped out of the SUV and flicked her fingers. Instantly the entire street froze. Paige gaped at the scene—a bouncing raver was suspended in midair; a couple was locked in a kiss; a slice of pizza was suspended, just as it was about to flop over onto some guy's shirt front.

Then Paige shook her head and scurried after Piper, who was sprinting for the alley. After all, their time was limited. You never knew when the magic was going to wear off, spontaneously unfreezing time and, perhaps, catching the witches in an awkwardly magic position.

When Piper and Paige plowed into the alley, they both gasped.

"You were right," Piper breathed. The frozen scene was terrifying. The girl was cringing against the alley's dirty brick wall, just as Paige had been earlier that night. And just like Josh, Stuart was looming over his prey with his right hand reared back. He sported the same glinting silver nails and malevolent muscle as Josh too.

"Okay, I've had just about enough of this," Piper said. "Explosion time."

But Paige grabbed Piper's arm.

"Wait," she said. "Think about this. Didn't it seem like Josh changed right after that oozy, tunnel thing sprang out of his head."

"Changed?" Piper sputtered. "Well, if you mean redirecting his violence from you to Phoebe, sure."

"No," Paige said, staring at Stuart's face, which was locked into a soulless grimace. He bore almost no resemblance to the compassion-ate social worker Paige had had lunch with just yesterday. "I mean, Josh was all about his heart-sucking thing. And then, as soon as the portal popped out of him, he was . . . back to the old Josh. He seemed pretty clueless about demons. He suddenly recognized Phoebe. And Phoebe suddenly had a change of heart too. She knew Josh. She must have seen the change."

"Paige, what are you saying?" Piper was star-ing at her sister in weary confusion.

"I'm saying . . . maybe Josh isn't a demon," Paige said slowly. "But he was possessed by one."

"I've gotta admit, the signs point to it, but . . ." Piper said. She rubbed her fingertips together and glanced at Stuart. Paige could tell Piper was just itching for a vanquish.

"So, here's the thing," Paige said. "Maybe Stuart's in the same fix—possessed by an evil something-or-other. If that's the case, that makes him an innocent too. So we can't vanquish him."

"But we could use him," Piper said, her eyes lighting up. "Maybe, if we exorcised the demon from Stuart, it could help lead us to Phoebe and Josh."

"Perfecto," Paige said, snapping her fingers. Then she looked worriedly at her watch. "But we're clocking in at about sixty seconds. I think an unfreeze is imminent, don't you?"

"Let's grab him," Piper said.

"And, uh, let's get help," Paige said nervously. She looked skyward and called, "Leo!"

Instantly a man-shaped swirl of white lights cascaded into the alley. Within a few seconds the orb corporealized into Leo. His shirt was rumpled and untucked and he was holding a half-eaten burger in his hand. Paige glanced at Piper and saw her sister give her husband an exasperated look. She could practically read Piper's thoughts: *Whatever happened to my knight in shining armor? Now he's just a humdrum husband!*

"Midnight snack," Leo said to Piper sheepishly. He tossed the burger into a Dumpster as soon as he saw the witches' drawn faces. "Where's Phoebe?"

"We'll explain later. Right now, we need your help," Paige said, nodding at Stuart. "We've got to take this dude home without letting him pull our heartstrings, if you know what I mean."

"What?" Leo sputtered. "*He's* the demon, now? What about Josh?"

"That would fall into the 'explaining later' category, sweetie," Piper said through gritted teeth. "For the moment, could you just orb this guy home and tie him up? I know taking hostages isn't our style, but if it's going to get Phoebe back, I'll try anything."

I've got to get out of this mess, Phoebe thought. *I'll try anything.*

She and Josh had been dumped by the silvery

portal about ten minutes earlier. After shaking
the shock out of their heads, they'd left the
chamber where they'd landed and gone to
explore.

Their findings were as bad as Phoebe had
feared.

First they'd crept through a passageway that
had taken them past a series of bed chambers.
The set-ups—low onyx beds with uncomfort-
able, wooden headrests, chamber pots, and
rough glass mosaics—were decidedly ancient.
Then, turning a corner into another hallway,
they'd found an open window hung with a
rough, papyrus shade. Peeking through, Phoebe
had seen a bustling city street filled with people
in rough tunics and sandals. Goats and pigs
were being herded down the street by black-
haired boys carrying long sticks. The buildings
across the street were made of sandstone and
fronted by Roman columns.

Since the building in which Phoebe and Josh
had landed was situated on a hill, they could see
much of the city. There was no sign of modern
life.

Anywhere.

In fact the signs of ancient life weren't even
complete. As they surveyed the scene, Josh suddenly gasped and grabbed Phoebe's arm.

"Look!" he whispered, pointing over the
city's roofs. In the distance Phoebe saw an
expanse of desert. And smack-dab in the middle

was a pyramid. Or at least . . . the beginnings of one. The giant structure was only half-finished. Its pointed top was a work-in-progress. Phoebe could even spot workers using ropes and pulleys to haul a giant block up the inclined pyramid wall.

"Ancient Egypt, it is," Phoebe said, looking at Josh with scared eyes.

"What did you *do* to me?" Josh blurted, glaring at her.

"Excuse me?" Phoebe sputtered. "What did I do to you? You're the one who spewed the time portal out of your *head*."

"What are you talking about?" Josh said. "One minute I'm on a lame date with this girl named Paige. The next minute she's in my apartment. She's changed clothes. And *you're* there beating my brains out, after which, I get sucked into some sort of vortex that spits me out a thousand years ago."

"Wait a minute," Phoebe sputtered. "Are you telling me you don't remember anything after your date with Paige? That was two days ago!"

"Or a thousand years in the future, depending on how you look at it," Josh said. "Okay, this is too freaky to even comprehend. So let's just try to figure out where we are and how to get back to San Francisco."

"Fine," Phoebe snapped, spinning around in irritation. She started to stalk down the hallway, but almost immediately, she skidded to a halt.

She heard a rustling at the other end of the hall—then the unmistakable shuffle of footsteps.

"Trouble," she squeaked over her shoulder to Josh. She glanced down at her gooey halter top and then at Josh's clunky sneakers. "Someone's coming. And we *definitely* don't fit in."

"Well, where are we supposed to hide?" Josh hissed desperately. Phoebe glanced around. He was right. There was nothing in this long, narrow hallway but sandstone walls and the single window they'd just been peeking through. Phoebe spun around desperately, then shrugged and dropped into a kung-fu ready stance.

"If there's nowhere to flee," she whispered to Josh, "gotta fight."

"What?!" Josh sputtered. "Phoebe Halliwell, boxing? What happened to the party girl I used to know?"

The past three years of Wiccan butt-kicking flashed through Phoebe's mind.

"A lot's happened since we broke up," she said to him dryly. Then she squatted and braced herself as the shadowy figure moving down the hallway came into view. As he stepped into the sunlight coming through the window, Phoebe gasped again.

If she'd needed proof that she and Josh were strangers in a strange land, here it was. The man, clearly a servant, was wearing a rough, vanilla-colored tunic tied at the waist with something that looked like woven brown hair. His own hair was black and curly, cascading down his back. In his rough hands, he held a reed basket filled with indigo cloth. Through his smiling lips Phoebe could see several missing teeth. And then an aroma—the definite scent of a man living in a predeodorant world—hit her hard.

Then she did a double take.

He's smiling, she thought. *He's looking straight at me and smiling like he's in the middle of a daydream. Or maybe he's trying to psyche me out. Maybe this is some sort of ancient Egyptian fighting tactic. A zen thing. Or a pre-zen thing.*

Well, if that's the case, I better take the first strike, Phoebe mused.

She balled up her fist, reared back, and threw a hard right hook at the guy's jaw.

"Whoa!" she screeched as she spun out of control. Losing her balance, she tumbled to the floor with a loud *splat*. She gaped at the servant's back as he continued to stroll down the hallway. Then she stared up at Josh who was biting his lip to keep from bursting out laughing.

"Nice shot, Phoebs," he said. "Like I said, I never thought you were the Mohammad Ali type."

"Hel-lo!" she said, lurching to her feet. "I connected. That is, I *would* have connected if his jaw hadn't passed right through my hand."

"Okay, *now* what are you talking about?"

"I'm talking about us not being exactly solid," Phoebe said. "Think about it, Josh. It's hundreds of years in the past. Which means, technically, we haven't been born yet."

"Are you saying we're ghosts?" Josh said, his eyes bulging.

"Or . . . preghosts," Phoebe said with a shrug. "After all, ghosts are usually dead, right? We can't be dead because we haven't yet lived."

Josh threw up his hands and collapsed against the stone wall.

"You could have fooled me, Phoebe," he said. "I mean, my memories of you dumping me a few years ago are pretty vivid."

"Oh, what an opportune time to bring *that* up," Phoebe sputtered. She began stalking down the hallway toward the doorway that the servant had entered. "Josh, I only dumped you because you went all cold and fishy on me. With no explanation, I might add."

As Josh struggled to keep up with her, Phoebe plowed through the doorway and burst into a large room. It looked like a banquet hall of some sort. It was lined with Italian-looking columns and the floor was inlaid with gold and lapis. It was beautiful!

"This must be a palace of some kind," Phoebe breathed, skidding to a stop.

"Wow," Josh blurted, almost knocking into her as Phoebe stopped in her tracks.

For one lovely instant, Phoebe had forgotten Josh was there. Now she gave him a baleful glare.

"There's a stairwell," she said, pointing to a majestic staircase on the opposite side of the hall. "Maybe that'll lead us out of here."

Josh hurried behind her as she descended the steps, gazing around for some more clues that might help them get back to her time. But she saw nothing.

When they reached the landing, the stairwell split into two. Phoebe shrugged and turned left, descending more steps. These were less majestic and more functional—encased in a low, clammy, stone tunnel.

"Another tunnel," she muttered. "Just my luck."

She and Josh went down, down, down. The air got darker and murkier. Oil torches flamed along the walls, staining the ceiling black and filling the air with icky, peaty smoke.

"Okay, this is clearly wrong," Phoebe said, biting her lip. She turned to Josh. She hated to rely on him but, well, he was all she had.

"Do you think we should turn back?" she asked.

"Or we could go toward the light down there," Josh said, pointing over Phoebe's shoulder. She turned and was surprised to see the tunnel culminate in a brightly lit, open room. There were voices murmuring inside and then, a piercing scream.

Phoebe started and headed toward the room.

I sure hope we're invisible to everyone here, she thought as she cautiously slipped inside the doorway.

Despite herself, she gasped out loud. But none of the people in the room—and there were several—turned to look at them. She and Josh were truly ghosts.

And it looked like the woman in the center of the room was about to become one too.

"Who *are* these people?" Josh blurted.

"Torturers," Phoebe said grimly.

The room, clearly an underground dungeon, was littered with devices made for pain. Phoebe saw a deep tub of water with a wide noose hanging above it. Next to that was a set of stocks, with holes cut in a slab of wood to immobilize a person's head and hands.

And in the middle of the dungeon was a giant spiked wheel. A beautiful woman with black hair and a sweaty, pale forehead was stretched onto the wheel. Her wrists, as well as her ankles, were tied with a leather thong. And two burly men with bare chests and Roman skirts were slowly tightening the leather straps. With each twist of the leather, the spikes dug deeper into the woman's flesh. Spots of blood stained her long, simple dress. Other men stood nearby. One held a whip. Another had a small mallet.

I don't even want to know *what that's for,* Phoebe thought, cringing at the woman's pain.

She was clearly in agony. But she didn't seem weakened or defeated. In fact she was quite the feisty torture victim.

She screamed a single word—in an ancient language that Phoebe didn't understand—at the ceiling. Then she shook her head defiantly.

"What is she refusing?" Phoebe whispered to Josh.

A deep voice spoke in the same unintelligible language. Phoebe looked up from the poor woman's writhing body to see a man step from behind the thick, wooden post of a gallows. He was a paunchy-gutted brute with a squashed nose and long hair that hung in greasy strings down his back. But he was clearly the noblest man in the room. His tunic was made of white silk edged in gold. His sandals snaked up his thick calves. And on his head, he wore a thin gold wreath.

"He must be a king or something," Josh said.

"What does he want from her?" Phoebe wondered.

"Catherine," the man intoned.

"Catherine!" Phoebe whispered. "Did you hear that?"

The man thumped his heart with his fist and made his demand again. Then he took a gold ring from a pocket in his tunic and shoved it roughly onto her left ring finger.

"Oh," Phoebe said dryly, as she realized what

the king was demanding. "Nice way to propose marriage!"

The woman—Catherine—gritted her teeth and stared defiantly at the man.

He squinted at her. Her silence was clearly a refusal. The king stared at her and spat on the floor. Then he jerked his head in a brusque nod.

Each of the servants gave their leather straps another violent twist.

"Arrrrgggh!" the woman wailed. Her screams were so loud that Phoebe covered her ears with her hands and shuddered. When Catherine's pain subsided into shuddering sobs, Phoebe looked up at Josh.

"And I thought I was afraid of commitment," she joked weakly. "What have we fallen into, Josh? And how are we going to get away from this awful place?"

Chapter
7

When Paige and Piper finally got back to the Manor, it was in the wee hours of Sunday morning. Leo and Cole had tied the writhing Stuart to a chair in the attic. And their hands were full.

"Thank goodness you're home," Leo said as the sisters bounded into the attic. "The guy kept winging out his claws and slicing through the rope we used to tie him up. Finally Cole and I had to resort to bars."

"You're handy around the house, Leo, I must admit," Piper said, raising her eyebrows at the metal rods coiled around Stuart's torso. "I wonder if there's a quiz that will give you extra points for that!"

While Leo rolled his eyes, the oblivious Stuart spotted Paige and Piper. His eyes went glassy.

"Paige," he said. "I'm so happy to see you again. God, you're even more gorgeous than you were when we went out—"

"Save it," Paige said, rolling her eyes and taunting Stuart. "I know what you're after. And you'll never get it. Cross my heart."

She made an X over her heart with her fingertip.

"*AARRRRGGGH!*" Stuart screamed, writhing so hard that the bars holding him down left bloody scratches on his arms. "Let me go. You will be sorry, should you not. You have no idea who you are dealing with."

"Oh, please," Paige said, shaking her head and turning to Piper. "These guys are like a broken record."

"'Broken' being the operative word," Piper spat. She planted herself in front of Stuart and bent over, thrusting her face into his. "That's what you're going to be unless you start talking."

She thumped lightly on Stuart's head with her knuckles.

"If you don't tell us what the deal is here, and what's happened to our sister," Piper said, "believe me, you're the one who's going to be sorry."

"*You* will be sorry," Stuart intoned. "Sorrier than the rest, even. You . . . you will be sorry."

Piper gazed deeper into Stuart's eyes and then recoiled. This guy was AWOL. His pupils were pinpricks. His voice was monotone. He was just a vessel for some implanted evil, which meant he was no help to them.

"Book of Shadows," she barked, straightening up and turning to Paige, Cole, and Leo. "I think this guy's a dead end. We have to figure out how to get Phoebe back ourselves."

"But first you have to explain to us what happened!" Cole sputtered. "Where is Phoebe?"

Paige turned to the guys and told them all about what had happened at Josh's apartment as Piper ran to the antique, Victorian lectern, where they kept the huge Book of Shadows. It wasn't until she began flipping through its thick pages that she was aware of her breathing. She was panting in short gasps. She could feel the blood roaring in her head, blocking out the sound of Paige's voice and Cole's angry, frustrated response. She was panicking, she knew it. But she couldn't help it. This was her darkest fear. After Prue's death, the thought of Phoebe in some unknown, perhaps dangerous, place was unbearable.

Piper started as she felt a warm, strong hand clasp her shoulder. She turned and locked eyes with her husband as he wrapped his arms around her.

"Piper," he whispered. "It's going to be okay. We'll get her back."

Piper bit her lip and nodded, allowing herself to sink into Leo's arms for a moment. Then she turned back to the Book and looked up at the ceiling. Or rather, she gazed up at the heavenly beings that she knew were watching from above it.

"Okay, girls," she said, imagining her mother, Grams, maybe even Prue, gazing down at her from that nebulous place where departed witches reside. "I'm going to need a little help here. Phoebe's in some other dimension, and we have to get her back—"

Before Piper could finish her sentence, the Book slammed open. The pages began to flip with a frantic whirring noise. Then, abruptly, they stopped. Piper found herself blinking down at a spell.

"To rescue a wytch from points unknown," read the ancient spell, "there must be a portal from one dimension to the next. Portals open at the exact moment of sunset or dawn; at midnight on a full moon; and at the first harvesting of millet or barley."

"Okay, millet fields are in pretty short supply in these parts," Paige said, peeking over Piper's shoulder. "And we've just missed dawn. And the next full moon is, like, nine days away."

Piper felt despair begin to seep into her mind. But she shook it away and turned to the group.

"Okay, Leo, you go to the Elders and see if they have some portal loophole," she said. Immediately Leo closed his eyes and disappeared in a storm of white lights.

"Paige," Piper said, glancing back at the Book of Shadows, "it says we need to burn some herbs and stuff while we say the spell that will bring Phoebe and Josh back. Can you go to the kitchen and grab them? We need arrowroot, sage, suet, mustard seed, and . . . uh, millet. And a few other items. Take a look."

Paige quickly jotted down the ingredients and hurried out of the attic.

Cole stood in the middle of the room, his fists clenched and his back rigid. Piper looked at him sympathetically. As helpless as she felt, she knew Cole must have felt much worse. Ever since Phoebe had used a potion during a life-and-death moment to take away Cole's demonic powers, Cole had been struggling. He hated not being able to use magic to help the witches fight off evil.

And Piper knew it must've been eating him up inside that he couldn't save Phoebe himself.

"What can I do?" he said to Piper through gritted teeth.

Piper searched her mind for a bone to throw to Cole. But the truth was, he *was* helpless. She shrugged.

"Can you copy down the spell from the Book of Shadows?" she offered meekly. She saw Cole's shoulders sag.

"Thanks for the busy work, sis," he said. "I know what you're saying. There's nothing I can do."

"I'm sorry," Piper choked.

"I know," Cole said, locking eyes with her. "Me too."

Piper had to look away and bite her lip. She

and Cole were in the same spot—terrified of losing Phoebe. And if they failed to bring her back, they'd be equally devastated.

"You'll be sorry," said a thick voice from across the attic. "You'll be sorrier, even than the rest of them. *You'll* be sorry . . ."

Piper squeezed her eyes shut and clamped her hands over her ears, trying to block out Stuart's demented rant. When, a moment later, she opened her eyes, Cole had bounded across the room. He was looming over Stuart, glaring at him menacingly.

"Who are you?" he demanded. "If you want to live you'll tell me now."

"Sorry . . ." Stuart said, his head bobbing up and down. "Sorrier even . . ."

"Quiet," Cole roared. He lashed out at Stuart, backhanding him across the face. Stuart's head snapped to the side and a tiny gash opened on his cheek. But he barely seemed to notice. He just gazed back up at Cole with those shiny, mad eyes and hissed, "Sorry . . . sorry . . . sorry."

"Cole," Piper cried. "Leave him. He's crazy. He doesn't know anything. And he's an innocent."

"Innocent," Cole blurted. "I don't think so. Somewhere in there lurks a demon. That demon has kidnapped my fiancée. And he's gonna talk!"

As he said this, he gave Stuart another backhanded blow.

"Ah!" Stuart cried. A gob of spit and blood flew from his mouth as Cole's fist connected with his face. "You'd best let me go. You'll be—"

"Sorry?" Cole countered. "Well, I'm willing to take that risk."

He gave Stuart another belt. And another.

"Cole, no!" Piper screamed.

At that moment Paige returned to the attic. She carried a metal bowl brimming with mossy green herbs and smelly powders.

"I've got it," she said. "Now wha-AHHHH!"

She was staring at Cole who was pummeling Stuart with mounting anger. Piper followed Paige's gaze and gasped.

A familiar silver rivulet was oozing out of Stuart's ear.

"Cole," Piper screamed. "Stop!"

But there was no stopping Cole. His rage was building with every blow.

"Who's"—*slap*—"sorry"—*thud*—"now?" he grunted between blows.

As the silver goo emerging from Stuart's head turned into a gush and the familiar tunnel began to form in the middle of the attic, Paige and Piper suddenly looked at each other.

"It's a portal!" they squealed at the same time.

Piper grabbed the bowl of herbs from Paige's trembling hands and ran over to the Book of Shadows. Paige dashed to a nearby table and searched wildly for some matches. Already the wind from the portal was beginning to howl around them, whipping their hair straight above their heads. Cole had stumbled backward and was staring at Stuart in bewilderment.

"Quick," Piper screamed, fighting to get to the Book of Shadows. "Before the portal closes! We have to do the spell!"

Phoebe didn't think she could stand it anymore. As she and Josh continued to cower just inside the dungeon's entrance, the king had ordered his servants to give Catherine's bindings two more wrenching twists. She'd screamed in agony until her strength had absolutely given out. But when the king had demanded her hand in marriage one more time, she'd gritted her teeth and shook her head.

"We have to do something!" Phoebe said, turning to Josh desperately. "We have to save her!"

"How, Phoebe?" he asked, his own eyes filled with pain. "We don't exist here. What can we do?"

"Oh, it's just like you to give up," Phoebe scowled, hugging herself as she watched the servants finally untie Catherine and haul her off the spiked wheel. Her robe was splattered with blood by now and her face was ghostly pale.

For a moment Phoebe thought she saw Catherine's eyes connect with her own.

Had she seen her? Was she so close to death that she was seeing ghosts? Phoebe reached out toward the woman and gave her a quavering smile.

But Catherine was looking right through her. Her eyes were glazed and her lips were moving, as if in prayer. The servants hauled her onto a stone platform and laid her there. Catherine continued to whisper to herself, pausing only once to glare defiantly at the man.

He gave his servants one more brusque order. They nodded and bowed.

"You must have been right," Phoebe whispered. "He's some sort of king or emperor."

"What did you mean by that?" Josh said. He was ignoring Catherine and staring at Phoebe. "'Just like me to give up.'"

"Well, you gave up on us, didn't you?" Phoebe snapped.

"Phoebe, *I'm* not the one who broke off our relationship," Josh said.

"Oh, yes, you were," Phoebe said. "You shut me out. You stopped talking to me. You got all cold and weird and wouldn't explain why."

Josh started to retort, but then he got a faraway look in his eyes and closed his mouth. His shoulders sagged and he shook his head.

"You're right," he said.

"I am?" Phoebe gasped. "I mean . . . of course, I am. But here's what I've always wondered, Josh. Why? We seemed like a good thing. I was falling for you in a big way. And then you changed."

"I know," Josh said. "I was falling for you too. And that's when I started waiting for the other shoe to drop."

"What do you mean?" Phoebe asked.

"Come on, Phoebe," he said. "Look at you. You're strong and sophisticated. You're this charisma queen."

"Thanks," Phoebe said, feeling herself flush. "But . . . why was this a problem?"

"You were bound to outgrow me," Josh said. "I was intimidated, I guess. Now I realize I was an idiot."

Phoebe was stunned. Josh was telling her she'd been too good to be true. And because of that, he'd sabotaged their relationship. Shaking her head in disbelief, Phoebe felt a surge of relief. Well, at least she knew what Josh's damage had been.

At the same time, her mind flashed on Cole. Cool, confident Cole, who never got weirded out, even when Phoebe levitated ten feet in the air and had psychic premonitions. Why hadn't she realized how lucky she was when she was back in San Francisco?

She gazed at Josh and realized, *I went after this guy. I plunged into this time portal to save him. Yeah, I was saving an innocent. But I was also haunted by an ex-boyfriend.*

And for that, I might have taken myself away from Cole forever.

So who's the saboteur now? she thought, wiping a tear from her eye. Then she took a deep shuddery breath and threw back her shoulders.

"No," Phoebe muttered, "I can't let it end like this."

She turned to Josh and clutched his arm.

"We have to figure out a way out of this," she said. "I need to get back home!"

But before Josh could react, Catherine's raspy voice filled the room. Phoebe turned to look at the tortured woman and gasped.

The emperor was standing above her, an enormous, curved ax in his hands.

But Catherine showed no fear as she spat words at her torturer. She was clearly still defying the king—perhaps even goading him into swinging the blade onto her weary neck.

"No!" Phoebe screamed. And she began to run toward the murderous king.

Back in the attic, Paige was flipping frantically through the Book of Shadows. The howling tornado emanating from the portal's mouth had whipped the Book closed and she couldn't find the spell.

Piper was hunched over the bowl of herbs, trying to prevent them from flying into the maelstrom.

"Hurry, Paige!" she screamed. "This could be our only chance!"

"I'm flipping, I'm flipping!" Paige cried, tearing at the Book in panic. "You just figure out how we're going to burn the herbs in this wind."

"Good point!" Piper screamed. Tears streamed across her cheeks. Then she had an idea.

"Paige," she cried, "grab the Book and orb us out of here!"

"What?!" Paige yelled. "You know my orbing is totally raw. We could end up anywhere."

"Do it," Piper ordered her. "Or Phoebe's going to stay wherever she's ended up . . . permanently!"

Paige grabbed the Book and Piper grabbed Paige. Then Paige squeezed her eyes shut and concentrated on the Manor's upstairs hallway. She just had to get them out of this room. Just a few feet. And everything would be fine.

Focus, she told herself.

"Project yourself," she whispered.

And then she felt the familiar airy sensation of her white lights, glimmering around her body like gossamer warmth.

Finally the brilliant shimmers stopped and Paige opened her eyes.

Uh-oh, she thought.

She was outside. She was more than outside. She was perched very high up in the air, straddling a drainpipe and bracing her high-heeled shoes on the shingles of a roof. Way down below, she could see Piper's SUV parked on the curb. And in front of her, clutching the chimney, was Piper.

"Paige," Piper said through gritted teeth, "we're on our roof."

"Okay, so instead of going one flight down the stairs," Paige said with a shrug, "I took us one flight up."

"Whatever," Piper said. She propped the bowl of herbs on her hip and sat awkwardly on the drainpipe. Then she inched her way toward Paige. "At least we're in close proximity. Find that spell. And did you get the matches?"

Paige yanked the matches out of the pocket of her trench coat, which she hadn't even had a chance to take off. Then she began whisking through the Book as if page-flipping was an Olympic event. In five seconds she'd found the spell.

"Got it!" she yelled.

"So do I!" Piper said, dropping a lit match into the bowl of herbs. Fragrant flames instantly filled the metal bowl. "Now I'll read the spell while you orb us in. And we'll just hope this procedure doesn't require the Power of Three!"

"Way to *not* put the pressure on!" Paige cried. She grabbed the bowl of smoking herbs from Piper while Piper swept the Book of Shadows into her lap and began reading:

Our sister lies
In points unknown;
Restore her to her loving home.
Bring her back
And please, intact,
Put an end to her aimless roam.

• • •

As she said the last word, Piper and Paige had orbed into the attic.

They gazed into the pulsating, predatory mouth of the tunnel that swirled in the center of the attic. It had grown so large now, Paige couldn't even see Cole and Stuart.

Piper peered deep into the tunnel. There was no sign of Phoebe.

"It's not working!" Paige screamed.

"Let's read it again," Piper yelled. "Say it with me. And Paige?"

"Yeah?" Paige cried, locking eyes with her sister.

"Make it count," Piper said. "This could be our last chance."

Paige gulped and squinted at the Book of Shadows, clutched in Piper's hands. And then they began to read.

Phoebe didn't stop to think.

She barely stopped to breathe.

And she certainly didn't remember that—in her ghostly state—she was as ineffectual as a poof of air.

She sprinted toward the emperor with her arms outstretched.

"Stay away from her!" she screamed as the man scowled at Catherine. He lifted his long-handled ax high over his head.

"Phoebe, no!" Josh cried.

Catherine murmured a last, angry oath, locking her feverish eyes with those of the evil king.

And as Phoebe leapt through the air, lunging at the emperor, he slammed the ax through Catherine's neck with a whistling *thwump*.

At exactly the same moment, Phoebe sailed through the king's body as if he were no more than a hologram. Then she tumbled across the dungeon floor.

"Nooooo!" she cried.

"Phoebe," Josh yelled, running over and scooping her up in his arms. He shot one terrified glance at Catherine's headless body, then whisked Phoebe out of the dungeon.

"I didn't save her," Phoebe said, incredulously, as Josh carried her through the hallway. "She was an innocent. And I didn't save her. She's . . . dead!"

"There was nothing you could do," Josh said, stopping to look down at Phoebe's weeping face. "You . . . wait a minute. Phoebe? Do you feel that?"

Phoebe looked up and gasped. She swallowed her tears as she said, "How could I not? That's a very familiar tornadoey feeling."

"Oh, no, not again," Josh cried as the ceiling began to open up. Sure enough, the great, silvery, mushy maw that had dumped them into ancient Egypt a few hours ago, had returned.

"No, this is a good thing!" Phoebe said,

clapping her hands together gleefully. "And I think I see my sisters' handwriting all over it."

"What are you talk—talk—AAHHHHH?" Josh cried, as the portal suddenly reached down and sucked him in with one giant, howling gulp.

"Don't forget me!" Phoebe yelled, leaping into the air after Josh. She felt the familiar gooey suction of the portal draw her into its mouth and, with a grateful feeling, saw the sandstone floor of the Egyptian palace disappear.

Then, of course, Phoebe and Josh commenced to screaming their way through the same roller-coaster ride they'd experienced the first time around, until . . .

Whoomp.

"Ow!" Phoebe squealed as she landed, nose-down on something hard and fuzzy. Sitting up painfully, Phoebe saw that she'd landed on an Oriental rug.

Grams's Oriental rug.

With a gasp Phoebe looked up and saw her sisters, breathing hard and gaping down at her sticky, silvery, gooey self with a combination of joy and horror.

They pounced on her with huge whoops of joy before Cole moved in to sweep Phoebe into his arms.

"I thought I'd lost you," he whispered into her neck.

"It worked!" Paige screamed.

"We did it!" Piper cried.

Phoebe gazed at her sisters over Cole's shoulder. Then she ran a hand over her goo-laden head and regarded Paige and Piper's tornado-tousled locks.

"I think it's safe to say," Phoebe said, "that I've never been happier for a bad hair day in my life."

Chapter

8

"Um, what just happened?"

Phoebe gave a start as she heard a strange voice break through her giddy family reunion. She disentangled herself from the arms of her fiancé and sisters and turned to see two very confused-looking guys staring at them. One was Josh, looking just as gooey and windswept as she was. The other, the one who'd spoken, was a stranger with a wash of mercurylike stuff on his face and neck.

And he was tied to a chair with a coil of rusty metal.

"Let me guess," Phoebe said, pointing to the bleary-eyed young nerd, "Josh Junior?"

"Yup, same deal," Paige said. "This is Stuart. He's another Kiss.commer."

"Hi," Stuart said. With his crooked glasses and nasal voice, he couldn't have seemed less demonlike if he tried.

"Okay, looks like we had a couple of cut-and-dry possessions here," Phoebe said. "I mean, as soon as that portal popped out of Josh's head, he was back to normal."

Then she flashed him a smile. "Maybe even better than normal," she said with a wink.

Stuart, however, was clearly weirded out.

"Okay, I get it now," he said nervously. "We went out for lunch, right, Paige? And then you must have slipped something into my orange juice to make me pass out. Now I'm being held hostage for some sort of demonic ritual. You're a pagan, right? Or Wiccan? Or a cult member? Please tell me you're not a Scientologist!"

"Ugh," Paige cried. "Not even. Listen, let's just get you untied and we'll explain everything, right, girls?"

She turned and shot her sisters an exaggerated wink.

"Memory spell?" Phoebe muttered to Piper.

"They'll never knew what hit 'em," Piper whispered back with a nod.

Twenty minutes later, the witches had de-gooed Josh and Stuart and brought them downstairs.

"Paige, this is the last time I'm going to ask you before I call a lawyer," Stuart whined. "What happened here?"

"Oh, Stu," Paige said, batting her eyelashes. "No reason to resort to lawyers. We have one right here. Of course, he's a *demon-lawyer*!"

"Aaaah! Aaaah! Aaaahhh!" Stuart shrieked.

"Paige!" Piper said, glaring at her sister. "No fair toying with the innocents just because all memory of this will be obliterated in a few seconds."

"What? You're going to brainwash me?" Stuart squeaked. "Aaaah! Aaaaaah! Aaaah!"

"Oh, puh-leeze," Phoebe said, clamping her hands over her ears. "Can we just say the spell? I can't stand the screaming."

"All together now," Piper said, holding a piece of paper up. Paige and Phoebe crowded next to her. En masse, they read:

> *Let memories of these events*
> *Cease to even be past tense.*
> *Wipe the slate as clean as air*
> *Let no recollection haunt them, ne'er.*

A sweet-smelling breeze skimmed over Josh and Stuart. When these gentle spells took effect, Phoebe always imagined one of her Wiccan ancestors sweeping through the room, blowing a kiss. Peace immediately washed over Stuart and Josh's troubled faces. It made it all the more ironic that people like Stuart thought of Wicca as a dark art.

"How did I get here?" Stuart said, grinning slyly at Paige as he pushed his dark-rimmed glasses farther up the bridge of his nose. "Paige, you little minx. Did you invite me in after our lunch date?"

Phoebe slapped a hand over her mouth to keep from guffawing as Paige gave her a scathing glare. Then she hooked her arm through Stuart's and marched him to the front door. When she opened it, she saw that a cold February rain had begun to fall.

"Stuart, I guess my announcement gave you a little shock," Paige said, gazing down at her—surprisingly short—suitor.

"Announcement?" he said.

"Yes, you know that I'd love to go out with you again," Paige said, "but unfortunately I've been called."

"Called?"

"Oh, yes," Paige said, clasping her hands and looking angelic. "I think missionary work will be so rewarding, don't you? I mean, even if Colombia is a little dangerous these days."

"Well . . . good luck with that!" Stuart stuttered, groping for the doorknob. "Great lunch, Paige. Nice knowin' ya."

"Bye!" Phoebe called, wrinkling her nose at Stuart as he hightailed it out of there.

"Phoebe!" Josh said. "It *is* you. What . . . are you and Paige related somehow?"

"Here we go again," Piper said, rolling her eyes.

"Sisters," Phoebe said to Josh as Paige and Piper melted out of the room. She couldn't help but grin at Josh's cute, confused face. "Long story."

"Ahem!"

Phoebe started and spun around to see Cole on the bottom step of the stairwell. He was glaring at Josh with a venom Phoebe hadn't seen since his Belthazor days. Normally Phoebe had no patience for jealousy but, after all that had happened in Egypt with Josh, she felt nothing but grateful for her devoted sweetie. She ran to the stairs and wrapped her arms around Cole's waist. He glanced down at her in surprise.

"And in addition to a new sister, I also have a new fiancé," she announced. Taking Cole's hand, she led him across the foyer to Josh. "Josh, Cole. Cole, Josh. An old . . . friend."

"Yeah?" Cole and Josh said at the same time.

"Yeah," Phoebe said, smiling at Josh. "At least I think we're friends."

"Yeah," Josh said, a grin slowly filling his face. "I'm not sure what's happened here, Phoebe, but knowing you, I think I'd best not ask."

Josh turned and extended his hand to a surprised Cole. "I will, however, congratulate *you*. You're a lucky man."

Then he headed to the front door and gave Phoebe a little wave.

"Call me if you want to explain any of this," he said to her. "Or just catch up. It's nice to see you again, Phoebe."

As he slipped out the door, Phoebe smiled to herself.

"Okay, do I want to know what happened to you on the other side of this time portal?" Cole asked, his face clouding.

"It's called closure, honey," she said, giving him a kiss. "It's a good thing, I promise you."

"Well . . ." Cole grumbled.

But before he and Phoebe could get into a whole "us" discussion, Leo suddenly orbed into the foyer.

"Phoebe!" he cried when he became corporeal. "You're back!"

He swept her up into a bear hug, then shook his head in relief.

"Paige and Piper to the rescue," Phoebe said, as her sisters came back into the foyer.

"Are . . . things cool with Josh?" Paige asked carefully.

"Totally," Phoebe said. "And those boys are definitely demon-free now."

"Yeah, but I'm thinking they might not be the last of them," Piper said. "All we know about this demon is that it's capable of possessing more than one man."

"Yeah," Paige said worriedly. "Which means we'd better find the original demon."

"Well, maybe Phoebe has some clues," Leo said. "After all, you went through the demon's time portal."

Phoebe shuddered as she suddenly recalled the grisly beheading she'd witnessed just before being sucked out of the alternate dimension.

Swallowing painfully, she nodded.

"I've got a name and address," she offered. "Catherine. Ancient Egypt."

"That's all you got?" Piper said with disappointment. "Phoebe, what were you doing down there?"

"Ever heard of that movie, 'Witness to the Execution'?" Phoebe countered. She couldn't keep her voice from trembling just a bit.

"Oh," Piper said softly, putting a hand on Phoebe's shoulder. "I'm sorry, sweetie."

"It's okay," Phoebe said. "Let's just get back to the attic and hit the Book of Shadows. I want to see if we've got anything on Catherine."

A half hour later, Phoebe at last found what she'd been looking for. It was in the slim, non-pagan section of the Book of Shadows.

"Aha!" she cried. "She was *Saint* Catherine."

"We're dealing with saints now?" Paige said. She glanced up from her laptop, where she'd been surfing Kiss.com for suspicious-looking characters. Piper was been scrying while Leo and Cole were studying other books on demonology from the Halliwells' library.

"I guess we are," Phoebe said, "because this story fits what I saw perfectly."

As her family gathered around her, Phoebe cleared her throat and began to read.

"'Catherine of Alexandria was a princess living

in fourth century, Roman-occupied Egypt,'" she
read. She stopped reading and looked at Piper
and Paige. "That's exactly where we must have
been. We were in a palace in a busy city. I saw some
Roman-looking architecture. But also . . . there
were pyramids-in-progress right outside the
window."

"Some vacation," Paige said dryly. "Read on."

"'The Roman emperor, Maxentius, demanded
Catherine's hand in marriage,'" Phoebe continued. "'When the pious princess refused him, he
attempted to torture her into submission.
Among the devices in his arsenal was a spiked
wheel, which was forever after called a
Catherine Wheel. Finally Maxentius beheaded
the princess. From her neck flowed milk, rather
than blood. And immediately a chorus of angels
came to steal Catherine's body away for a
proper burial on Mount Sinai."

"Harsh!" Paige said. "You saw that, Phoebe?"

"I didn't see the milk," Phoebe said. "But
believe me, I saw enough to connect the dots.
Now here's the really scary part. 'Maxentius, in
executing the saint, became doomed. When he
died a few years later, he became the ephemeral
demon, Lupercalus."

"Lupercalus?" Leo piped up. "That's ironic.
Lupercalia was the ancient name for February
fourteen."

"Sick sense of love, this guy," Phoebe said,
shaking her head.

Paige stood up and drifted over to Phoebe, peering over her shoulder at the Book. Gently she reached out and ran her finger over a drawing of a beautiful, black-haired woman. At the bottom of the page was a picture of a burly man in a Roman tunic. "Maxentius, Emperor of Rome," was its caption, written in florid, curly handwriting.

And finally, beneath a drawing of a ghostly wolf, was the word, "Lupercalus."

"Why the wolf?" she wondered out loud.

"Latin," Cole explained. "*Lupo* is the root for Lupercalus. Means wolf."

"Okay, smartie," Paige shot back with a smile. "Then explain this one: What's an ephemeral demon?"

"An ephemeral demon exists—or doesn't, depending on how you look at it—in the ether," Cole said. "Some catalyst can make him temporarily corporeal. And then he'll stay that way as long as he's accomplishing his mission."

"His mission being? . . ." Phoebe wondered.

"Revenge against Catherine," Piper said suddenly. "Of course. He's taking out his rage on single women, through men that he possesses."

"The men who date Paige," Phoebe pointed out.

"What?" Paige gasped. "You think this has something to do with me?"

"Paige, Josh and Stuart's last nondemonic

memory is of their dates with you," Piper said. "Now do you think that's a coincidence?"

"But what does that mean?" Paige said. "Am I possessed?"

Paige spun around in a panic and ran to a warped, cloudy mirror leaning against the attic wall. She stared into her own eyes, trying to detect something beyond her usual brown irises and mascara'd lashes. But she couldn't see a thing either because there was no demon lurking in her head or because tears had sprung to her eyes, clouding her vision.

"Paige," Leo said, walking over and patting her on the shoulder. "Don't worry. Those guys were clearly possessed and you're clearly not."

"No," Cole said brusquely, walking over to Paige with his arms crossed over his chest. "She's probably a conduit."

"A what-o-it?" Paige said, sniffling a little and leaning her head on Leo's shoulder.

"A conduit," Cole said. "I knew a few demons in the old days who got around that way. Sneaky devils."

"Literally," Piper said. "So, what . . . . our demon is going through Paige, but not hanging around inside of her?"

"That's about the size of it," Cole said.

"Ew!" Paige screeched. "But how does he get in? How does he get out? I can't take a shower until this is over with!"

Chime.

"Have you ever noticed that the door always rings at the *most* inopportune times in this house?" Phoebe said.

"Oh, God," Paige groaned suddenly. "What time *is* it?"

"Nine-thirty," Piper said looking at her watch. "Ugh, we've been up all night."

"That's Max!" Paige screeched. "We made a Sunday brunch date. And now it's Sunday. I completely blanked. Oh, I hate to have to blow him off."

"Why on earth would you blow him off?" Cole said. "Here's an opportunity! Can someone get the door and ask Max to wait in the conservatory?"

"I will," Piper said.

"No, wait!" Cole said, his eyes glinting with an idea. "Leo, you get the door. We don't want Max to see Piper or Phoebe. They'll be spying later."

"Okay, Cole," Paige said as Leo headed downstairs. "Let's hit pause for just a minute here. What are you cooking up?"

"Simple," Cole said. "You go out with this Max guy. This is your second date, right? So either he's already been possessed through you and is coming back to eat your heart out, so to speak. Or the demon's going to possess Max on your date this morning. Whatever happens Phoebe and Piper will be there to see it. This could provide us with just the information we need."

"So you want Piper and Phoebe to come with and spy on us?" Paige said. "Cole, I *like* this guy. I don't want to risk infecting him with this demon! Ick. It's like I have a disease or something."

"Ah, remember when we were that naive?" Piper muttered to Phoebe with faux nostalgia. "Back before half our dates turned out to be green and scaly?"

"Or we were turned into baddies ourselves?" Phoebe said warmly. "All of this is just beginning for our Paige."

"This isn't funny!" Paige cried.

"No, no, you're right," Phoebe said, stifling her giggles. "Oh, I'm sorry, honey. I know it feels rotten. But look at it this way: If you don't go out with Max we may never figure out how to exorcise this demon, which would pretty much make you a big old Dating Don't, you know? Better to figure out a way out of this a.s.a.p."

"And let's not forget the innocents with lives at stake," Piper said, rolling her eyes. "I mean, I think Paige's social life is as important as anybody's, but it's not exactly life and death."

Paige went a shade paler than usual, then nodded weakly.

"Okay, okay, I'll do it," she sighed. "But look at me! I'm a mess. Would it be so wrong to do a magic makeover? It's not personal gain if it's in the name of innocent-saving, is it?"

Phoebe raised her eyebrows at Piper.

"That settles it," she said. "This girl's definitely a Halliwell. And I just happen to know a clean-up spell that will get us pretty in a jiffy."

"Why am I not surprised by that?" Piper remarked dryly. "All right, Ms. *Jiffy*. Charm away."

Chapter

9

Max took Paige to a quiet little restaurant on one of San Francisco's steepest streets. It was a romantic spot called Maison, tucked into the basement of a ramshackle row house. As soon as they walked in, Paige looked around the tiny dining room and sighed with delight—the place looked like her dream apartment. It was furnished in shabby, flea-market finds, with mismatched china and tarnished, silver candlesticks on every table.

And Phoebe's little spell had dressed her perfectly for the place. She was wearing a long, semisheer skirt and a silk, bronze-colored twin set. Very Sunday morning in the city.

Max whispered something to the host when he and Paige arrived. And by the time they sat down at a cozy, corner table, champagne-free bellinis were waiting for them.

Max held his flute of orange juice up and toasted Paige. "I know it's only been a few days, but . . ." and then Max looked down at his plate. "Well, let's just say, you've been on my mind since our last date."

"Likewise," Paige said, feeling her cheeks flush. She looked at her chipped plate and wondered where this giddy feeling was coming from. *It's so strange,* she thought, *that all the other guys were such duds and this guy is so . . . perfect. Attraction is so bizarre that way.*

As soon as the giddy thought crossed her mind, Paige felt guilt wash over her.

So, of course, what do I do? she asked herself. *I subject my new beau to demonic possession. Oh, yeah, average second-date stuff.*

Or, she thought darkly, *I'm subjecting myself to possession. Maybe Max has already been posessed by Lupercalus.*

Paige gazed at her date. He was buttering the stack of toast the waiter had brought for the two of them. Just looking at Max gave Paige a trembly feeling. His skin was so tan, with just the right smattering of laugh lines. His hair was glossy, falling onto his forehead with a combo of polished handsomeness and Hugh Grant floppiness. He was dressed perfectly too in a cool, linen shirt and wonderfully worn jeans.

But still, a demon could make himself as gorgeous as he wanted to, couldn't he? Paige thought nervously. She sighed and broke off a bite of toast of her own. Being a nascent witch gave one such an insecure feeling! She wished she had her sisters' experiences. They could probably pick out a demonic date within five minutes.

Or, Paige thought, shooting a furtive glance across the dining room, *maybe not.*

Piper and Phoebe had just been seated at a table about fifteen feet away. They looked perfectly breezy—Piper wore capri pants and a peasant blouse and Phoebe was in hip-hugging jeans. They were also making a big show of peeking at Paige over their menus and seemed to be giggling to themselves.

Wonderful, Paige thought, biting into an asparagus spear ruefully. *I guess I'm on my own here. I wonder what the heck those two are laughing about?*

"Okay, okay," Phoebe was saying, as the waiter brought her a dainty cup of coffee. "My turn. My most embarrassing date ever was . . . that guy who took me to a Bon Jovi concert and played air guitar throughout the entire thing. I was crawling under my seat."

"Literally," Piper gasped. "I remember you coming home with gum in your hair."

"Ew! Of course that was preferable to a goodnight kiss with that guy," Phoebe said.

"And let's not forget all the boyfriends who turned out to be demons," Piper said, taking a pensive slurp of her tea. "Kind of brings that 'not knowing who to trust' doctrine to a whole new level, doesn't it?"

"Of course demon-dating worked out for me," Phoebe said with a sly grin. "But I wouldn't wish it on Paige. Poor thing. What's going on over there?"

Piper peeked over her menu, then rolled her eyes.

"All's gaga on the western side of Maison," she said. "I've got to admit . . . Max doesn't have that demony look about him. But at least we all got a nice brunch out of this stake-out."

Piper fished a warm and oozy chocolate croissant out of the bread basket that she and Phoebe had ordered. Then she shook her head.

"Wow. Can you even remember what it's like to be on a first date?" she asked, taking a huge bite of the croissant.

"The excitement? The swooning?" Phoebe said. "The wondering through an entire conversation if there's spinach in your teeth?"

Then she rolled her eyes.

"Oh, yeah," she said dryly. "I miss it desperately."

I wonder if there's spinach in my teeth, Paige was thinking as she polished off the last of her eggs Florentine. *God, I hope not.*

Between her first bite of breakfast and her last, Paige had decided she adored Max Wolf.

And she'd decided there was no way a dude like this could be a demon.

"I know you're probably thinking I'm an ego-maniac," he'd said a few minutes ago. "Aren't all politicians that way?"

"Well . . ." Paige had said. "They don't start out that way but something about the system corrupts, doesn't it seem?"

"I know," Max said with a sigh. "But I can't get certain things I've seen out of my head, Paige. I'm a public-aid lawyer. Every day I see this cycle of poverty that seems impossible to break."

"But we have to try," Paige and Max said at the same time. Paige laughed incredulously. Then she stared into Max's sweet, brown eyes.

"This is the first time I've ever met someone who cares as much about these issues as I do," she breathed.

Max stared back at her with such intensity, Paige felt a dizzy spell wash over her.

Is this that love-at-first-sight, bonked-on-the-head feeling? she wondered. *Gee, I never thought it would be so . . . literal.*

Finally Paige had to drag her eyes off of Max's face and put a hand to her forehead.

"Whew," she whispered, "that was a little intense."

"I felt it too," Max breathed. "Part of me wishes I could steal you away. Or at least force you to forsake all others."

Paige giggled at his old-fashioned language and Max rolled his eyes in embarrassment.

"But I know I can't ask you to do that," he said. "I'm sure you're the belle of the Kiss.com ball."

"Oh . . . not really," Paige said, thinking guiltily of her packed Palm Pilot. Then she shot a glance in Phoebe's direction. What had Phoebe told her? Be elusive and a little aloof?

"I could cancel my other dates, Max," she blurted.

Whoops, Paige thought as the words shot out of her mouth. *That wasn't exactly aloof. But who cares? Max and I clearly have one of those electric connections. Do we really have to play games?*

"Paige, I'm flattered," Max said. "But . . . you shouldn't."

"Oh . . ." Paige said. Humiliation began to curdle the hollandaise in her stomach.

"Not . . . yet," Max said shyly. "I don't want you to rush to commit to me. You should play the field. Be really sure. And when you're ready, I'll be here."

Paige nodded slowly, trying to figure out whether Max was the most gallant guy on earth, or was subtly dissing her.

But before she could say anything else, their waiter brought Max back the check and his credit card. Max scanned the bill, then signed the dotted line with a fountain pen he'd pulled out of his shirt pocket. Paige squinted at Max's upside-down handwriting. Something about the signature looked familiar. The letters slanted and curled around each other in antique-looking flourishes. It was beautiful. . . .

Suddenly Paige gasped.

She stared at the fountain pen in Max's manicured fingers. And she flashed back to the attic.

The Book of Shadows page she'd been studying that morning filled her mind like a vision. And what she saw were the words, *Maxentius. Lupercalus.*

Then Paige's mind flashed on Cole. "*Lupo* is the root for Lupercalus," he'd said that morning in the attic. "Means wolf."

Paige could feel her heart beating in loud, panicky thuds. Her mind was racing.

She lifted her eyes from Max's fountain pen to his smooth, untroubled face and his piercing, amber eyes. His *hypnotizing* eyes.

Maxentius. Lupercalus, Paige thought, feeling a sheen of sweat break out on her upper lip.

Max.

Wolf.

Paige's hands went clammy. Instinctively she looked around the restaurant for an escape route. But she was sitting in the corner. She'd have to get around Max to dash out of the restaurant.

And besides, if she dined and dashed, the demon would know that she was onto him.

Paige shook her head. As much as the proof was

right before her eyes, in ink on the brunch bill, it was still hard to wrap her brain around the painful fact that she'd been duped. Hugely duped.

And if she didn't play her cards right, she was doomed.

So Paige put on her game face. The same one she used when trying to placate violent husbands or angry judges in family court. She added a dash of flirtation, and batted her eyelashes subtly.

"Oh, I'm sure about you already, Max," she said.

Yeah, sure that you're the biggest jerk I've ever dated, she thought.

"But, you're probably right," she continued. "We should take things slowly. After all, a connection like ours doesn't come along that often."

"Maybe only once every few centuries," Max said with a teasing smile.

Oh, that does it, Paige thought. *I am so onto you.*

"In fact," Paige said sweetly as she got out of her chair, "I think I need some time just to . . . you know, think about things. I think I'll walk home."

"In the rain?" Max said, his eyebrows raised.

"I love walking in the rain," Paige said. "You know, like the song says. But thanks for brunch. It was . . . enlightening."

"For me, as well," Max said, rising to his feet and taking Paige's right hand. Slowly, he lifted it to his lips, then planted a gentle kiss on her index finger.

Paige's head snapped back as she felt a burst of electricity shoot up her arm. It was like a current that ended in her heart, making her hunch over in a spasm of . . . not pain, exactly. More like surprise.

Paige snatched her hand away from Max and pressed it to her side, hoping he wouldn't be able to see how much she was trembling. Then she smiled tremulously and sidled past Max. She breathed a sigh of relief as she saw her sisters take one look at her, then throw some money on their table and stand up.

She left the restaurant without looking back and took a few wobbly steps down the sidewalk. The rain had subsided to a foggy mist. Paige had to squint to see through it, so she didn't know Phoebe had walked up behind her until she felt her hand on her shoulder. Paige jumped and squealed.

"Oh, I'm so glad to see you," Paige whimpered, throwing her arms around Phoebe's shoulders. Then she pulled back and stared into Phoebe's frightened eyes.

"It's him," Paige breathed. "Max is Lupercalus."

"We figured when you suddenly dashed out of there," Phoebe said. "Piper went to grab the car."

No sooner had the words left her mouth than Piper skidded up in the black SUV.

"Home, Jeeves?" she called through the passenger window.

Paige and Phoebe tumbled into the car. By the time Piper pulled up to Halliwell Manor fifteen minutes later, Paige had recounted the entire breakfast for them.

"I'm sure Dr. Laura would have something to say about this," Paige said glumly as they walked into the foyer. She glanced into the mirror and fluffed out her rain-dampened hair. "I mean, how perverse is it that all my nondemonic dates bored me to tears. And the one guy I liked turns out to be a Roman emperor with a king-sized grudge. Do I have bad taste in men or what?"

"Or what!" Piper declared. "Paige, think about it. If Lupercalus could somehow jerryrig you so that you turned all your dates into killing machines, don't you think he could manipulate the dates themselves? He hexed you!"

"Why would he do that?" Paige retorted, slumping back against the wall next to the hall mirror. "I mean, once I made eye contact with the guys, the deed was done, right?"

"Yes, but had you liked any of them, you might have stopped your dating rampage," Phoebe pointed out.

"Excuse me?" Paige said. "Rampage is such a desperate word. Could we just go back to calling it 'playing the field'?"

"Didn't you say that Max urged you to keep dating at brunch?" Piper said.

"Um, yeah, come to think of it," Paige said.

"Of course he did," Phoebe said, giving Paige a squeeze. "Keeping you on the lame-date treadmill would produce an army of bloodsuckers for Lupercalus. It was the perfect plan."

"It *was* the perfect plan," Piper said, biting her lip. "And now we have to figure out how to thwart it."

Chime.

"You were right about the crazy timing of that doorbell," Paige said to Phoebe.

And sure enough, when Paige swung the door open, there was Max, a stiff, fake smile on his face.

"Hi!" Paige blurted brightly, planting herself firmly in the doorway. "Max! Uh . . . miss me already?"

"Of course, Paige," Max said, neatly sidestepping her to come into the foyer. "But that's not why I'm here."

"Oh?"

Max turned at the sound of Piper's voice. She was stationed at the living-room door. And directly across from her, Phoebe manned the dining-room door.

"So why *are* you here?" Phoebe asked. "Just sisterly curiosity. I'm Paige's big sister, Phoebe. And this is Piper."

"Nice to meet you," Max said distractedly. Then he gave Paige a sidelong look. "I, uh, forgot my umbrella. I swear, I've outfitted half of San Francisco with my cast-off rain gear. But this time, since it provided an excuse to see you again, I decided to go after it."

"Oh," Paige said flatly. Then she looked around the foyer. "Um, I don't see it. Did you leave it in the conservatory?"

Max gave Paige another hard look.

"Ah, yes, I think I did," Max said. "I remember where it is. I'll just go look."

Max smiled politely at Phoebe as she stepped aside to let him pass. When he'd crossed through the dining room into the plant-filled conservatory, Phoebe turned to her sisters.

"Okay, bird in hand," she whispered. "Now what do we do with him?"

"I don't know!" Piper said. "We haven't had a chance to do any research. No spell, no potion, no nothin'."

"Except that exploding finger of yours," Paige said. "Better try it out."

"Better not."

Paige froze as she heard Max's voice behind her. In fact, she almost *felt* it. The moment Max spoke—in a voice that was lower and more sinister than his normal one—her hair stood on end. She spun around to see Max looming by the dining-room door. Needless to say, he wasn't holding an umbrella. He did, however, have a handful of crackling electricity and he was rearing back to wing it at Paige.

Paige screamed in terror and cringed as the blue-hot energy zinged through the air. Then she felt the now-familiar sensation of her body orbing into nothingness. It was how her magical self reacted to threat, no conscious will necessary.

By the time Paige orbed back into place, the energy ball had hit the wall behind her with a crackling explosion.

"Ha!" Piper yelled, flicking her hands in Max's direction.

Max was unphased. His eyes had turned acid-yellow, bulging with venom. An almost-invisible force field—ice blue and sparking like a live wire—had instantly formed around his body. The shield bounced Piper's explosive magic right back in her direction.

"Watch it," Phoebe screamed, leaping across the foyer in one huge bound. She caught Piper around the waist and together the two crashed to the floor. The explosion hit the mirror on the wall right behind the spot where Piper had been standing.

"Okay, so he's got wolf eyes, electric ammo, and a force field," Phoebe cried. "But we have the Power of Three."

"Or do you?" Max said. "Remember I've got a conduit in your love-hungry sister's head. Test me and I'll show you what else my little pathway can do for her."

With that, Max stared at Paige. His rheumy, animalistic eyes glowed. Suddenly Paige felt pain sear her brain like a branding iron. But it wasn't a physical pain she felt. No, it was the anguish of Lupercalus's victims.

Paige's own life melted away as Max filled her head with the feelings of Carla Janowski. The woman's last few hours flashed through Paige's mind in searing, warp speed. In quick succession, Paige experienced all of Carla's emotions. She ached for affection. Then she was hopeful. Then giddy with a new crush.

Then Paige felt herself experience Carla's final minutes. She crumpled to the foyer floor, hugging herself tightly, rocking back and forth and weeping softly. Paige felt fingers of passion shooting through her. A kiss. This must have been the end of Carla's date.

And then horror. Excruciating pain. Paige clawed at her chest as she felt the phantom slicing and dicing of one of those silver claws.

"Stop it!" Phoebe screamed. The noise jolted Paige out of her nightmare slightly, but Max's mental onslaught had left her incredibly weak. She was only dimly aware of Phoebe scrambling to her feet and running at Max, her fists poised for a fight.

Max howled, turning his attention from Paige to zing his hand in Phoebe's direction. This time his electric weapon took the shape of a long, snaky coil. It caught Phoebe across the neck and knocked her, gasping, to the floor. Paige could see Phoebe's feet twitching slightly as she lay still.

She also felt Lupercalus's emotional vise completely release her aching head. She slumped forward, clutching her temples. Just before she blacked out, she saw Max run across the foyer. As he did, a gust of wind suddenly filled the hallway.

A portal sprang up from the Oriental rug, unleashing its wild flurry of wind, chaos, and excruciating noise.

Of course, Paige thought weakly. *It's the ephemeral demon's favorite highway—the time portal.*

Max took a flying leap into the tunnel's mouth, which closed around him like a gooey, Venus flytrap.

And finally, when the tunnel disappeared, Paige let go. Everything went black.

Chapter
10

"Paige!" Phoebe screamed. Painfully, she picked herself up off the floor and went to her sister's side.

"Phoebe? What's going on?"

Phoebe looked up from her sister's comatose face to see Cole, barreling down the stairs, his face drawn and white with fear. Leo was right behind him.

"You were right," Piper said. "Max was Lupercalus and he pulled a number on Paige's head. She was in so much pain, she passed out."

Cole kneeled down next to Phoebe, who was cradling Paige's head, while Leo placed his hands on Paige's forehead. After a few seconds of his healing glow, Paige's eyelids fluttered open. She coughed and shook her head back and forth.

"Paige," Leo said, waving his hand before her bleary eyes. "Are you in there? Snap out of it."

He stared into her eyes for a moment, then froze.

"What's wrong?" Cole said. "Here, let me try."

Cole leaned over Paige and put a finger to her chin, turning her face so that her eyes met his.

"You blacked out for a minute, sis," he said. "But you're okay, now. I promise. How many fingers?"

Cole held up three fingers, then looked into Paige's eyes for a sign of recognition. Paige blinked slowly and winced.

"Three," she croaked.

Cole didn't respond. In fact, he and Leo both sat perfectly still as Paige sat up, shook her head once more, and then popped to her feet.

"Wow, that glow thingy is amazing," she said brightly.

Leo and Cole continued to sit on the floor in silence.

"Uh, guys?" Phoebe said.

"Cole, Leo!" Piper said, snapping her fingers. "Where did you guys go?"

Leo raised his right hand.

And it began to change. At first the change was subtle. His skin went a little gray. His fingers seemed to lengthen. But then, Leo's hand took a shape that was becoming all too familiar to the witches.

The ropy, metallic muscles.

The elongated, predatory fingers.

And worst of all, the eruption of those long, glinting talons.

Leo leapt to his feet and held his hand aloft. Then he began to stalk toward his wife.

"Leo?" Piper said timidly. "Okay, what's going on here?"

"Oh, no," Phoebe said, circling Leo carefully. "Lupercalus's attack must have put some extra-strong mojo into Paige's head. He's come through the conduit and possessed Leo!"

"Um, Phoebe?" Paige said. She sidled up to her sister and tapped her on the shoulder.

"Not now, Paige," Phoebe whispered. "We've got a situation here. Geez, I can't believe even a possessed Leo would turn on his own wife. What a blow!"

"Phoebe!" Paige yelled. "Watch out!"

Phoebe spun around just in time to see her own sweetheart bearing down on her. And he was wielding a brand-new, extra-shiny claw.

"What a blow," Piper simpered. Then she returned her attention to Leo.

"Honey?" she said to him. "You already have my heart. Trust me, you don't need to go any further."

"Cole!" Phoebe was saying as her fiancé backed her against the foyer wall. "Please! Don't make me kung fu you."

"You'll . . . be . . . sorry," Leo droned, moving a step closer to Piper.

"I will have my revenge," Cole sneered, lunging at Phoebe with his claws.

"Oh no, not this again," Paige complained as she looked back and forth between the two couples. "I can't take it anymore."

And with that, she reached out her hand and ordered, "Candlestick!"

One of the heavy brass candlesticks that always sat on the dining-room table suddenly orbed into Paige's hand. As soon as it became solid in her fist, she reached up and conked Leo on the head with it.

"Leo!" Piper cried. Then she gazed at Paige in shock.

"You just bonked my husband," she said.

"Yeah, just before you reached a new, lethal level of intimacy," Paige said.

"Um, you have a point," Piper said. Then she jumped as Phoebe whooped on the other side of the foyer.

"Hi-yah!" she cried, suddenly shooting her leg in a high circle kick and knocking Cole's hand away from her chest, where he'd been just inches away from digging in for her heart. With Cole unbalanced, Phoebe grabbed his claw and wrenched it behind his back. Cole struggled mightily, accidentally slashing one of Phoebe's cheeks with a talon.

"Phoebe!" Piper cried. Then, instinctively, she flicked her hands out and froze Cole in mid-writhe.

Phoebe fell back against the wall and sank to the floor, cupping her cheek.

"He hurt me," she said incredulously.

"It's not him," Paige said, trying to comfort Phoebe. "You know that."

Piper merely stood over Leo and stared at him sadly. When he'd passed out, his clawed hand had receded and now he looked like himself again—vulnerable and sweet.

"Piper," Paige said, "I know that look. It's the, 'Aw, Leo's so cute when he's sleeping look.' And you've got to shake it off! When your husband comes to, he's going to be Lethal Leo. That is, until we figure out how to exorcise Lupercalus in some way that doesn't get us sucked into ancient Egypt."

"She's right, Piper," Phoebe said sorrowfully. "For now, we've got to stash our sweeties in a place where they'll do no harm."

"The basement," Piper declared. "There are bars on the window and a bolt lock on our side of the door."

"Yup," Phoebe said. "Perfect. Let's move 'em before Cole unfreezes."

"You up for orbing these guys down there?" Piper said, giving Paige a skeptical glance.

"Sure!" Paige said defensively. "Although, I think I'll do my 'fetch' routine. I've had more practice at that."

Nervously, she went into the basement with Phoebe and Piper at her heels. Paige stood in the middle of the messy room, littered with old tools and Prue's photo-developing equipment, and squeezed her eyes shut.

"Cole!" she shouted. An instant later, Cole shimmered into the basement, practically knocking Paige over.

"Cool!" Paige cried.

"You've *got* Cole," Piper said. "Now, Leo."

"I said, 'cool,'" Paige said, glaring at her sister. But then she recomposed herself and called out Leo's name. Lo and behold, her brother-in-law orbed in as well. The Halliwells gave each other a quick glance, then high-tailed it up the stairs.

"Book of Shadows," Phoebe said as she reached the top of the stairs. "Now!"

She and Paige hurried out of the kitchen as Piper slid the bolt lock into place. The minute the door locked, she heard a crash.

"And that would be Cole unfreezing," she whispered to herself. She cringed and pressed her ear to the door. Leo must have just woken up, too. She could hear him droning, "Sorry . . . you'll be sorry!"

Then Cole started bellowing, "Phoebe! Let me out of here! Phoebe!"

Piper gave the door a sharp tug to make sure the lock was secure, then spun around.

"Aahh!" she gasped. She was staring at two strangers.

Two men.

Two men with sharp, silver claws where their hands should have been.

"Paige!" Piper screeched. "Your dates are here!"

Then she threw up her hands to freeze the attackers before they could move in for her heart.

Phoebe and Paige skidded into the kitchen and gasped.

"Whoa!" Phoebe said. "Paige, how many guys did you go out with?"

"Just four!" Paige protested. "That's Charlie, my coffee date from the other day, and uh . . . uh . . ."

"You forgot the other guy's name?" Piper said, planting her fists on her hips. "Paige! You're fast."

"Am not," Paige retorted. "Just James! His name is James. Of course . . ."

Chime.

"Hmm, I wonder who *that* is?" Phoebe said, glaring at Paige. Paige glanced at the kitchen clock.

"Oh, that's right," she said sheepishly. "Sunday lunch with Alan, the media consultant. How could I forget? Don't worry. I'll get rid of him."

While Phoebe and Piper stood guard, Paige hurried to the front door, muttering as she went. "You'd think they never had a dry spell in *their* dating lives. Don't understand . . . so easy for them . . ."

Paige was still in vent mode when she opened the front door. And then she stared, her mouth hanging open.

There was Alan, the media consultant *and* Teddy, the E.R. doctor.

"Uh, hi guys," Paige stuttered. "Did I double-book? How incredibly . . . awkward."

Then Paige shut her mouth because she realized her dates didn't seem to mind in the slightest. They were simply standing on the porch, their eyes riveted to her.

And why didn't they mind? Because they'd become hypnotized the moment Paige opened the door and gaped at each of them.

"Noooo!" Paige groaned, dashing back into the kitchen with her dates—claws out—in hot pursuit.

"Piper!" Paige cried. "One, please don't be mad. Two, freeze these jokers!"

Piper turned away from Bachelors 1 and 2 to put an instant freeze on 3 and 4.

"This is ridiculous," Phoebe said. "Why didn't we realize Paige shouldn't have answered the door! And Paige? We'll deal with the 'double date' later, okay?"

"An honest mistake," Paige grumbled, crossing her arms irritably.

"Let's orb these guys into the basement and come up with a plan," Phoebe said.

Paige grabbed two of her Kissers by the frozen elbows and, crossing her fingers, orbed. When she opened her eyes, she was on the basement side of the door. Yes! Orbing back into the kitchen, she repeated the maneuver. But this time the boys unfroze as soon as they hit the basement steps.

"You'll be sorry," Alan growled.

"Inconstant love," Teddy roared.

"Eeek!" Paige squealed before orbing out of the basement. She landed back in the kitchen to the sound of her suitors banging fruitlessly on the door.

"Inconstant love," Paige muttered. "*Everyone's* a critic."

Then she stopped short.

"Wait a minute," she said, turning to face her sisters. "Love! That's what this is all about, right? Thwarted love. And revenge for it? So maybe the way out is to give the love that Lupercalus wants."

"So what do we do," Piper asked sarcastically. "Bake them a cake?"

"Well, I think we should start with the one you really *do* love," Paige countered. "Maybe if you shower Leo with affection, it'll knock the revenge demon out of him."

"Paige," Piper sputtered, "that's . . . that's crazy!"

"Is it?" Phoebe said, putting a hand on Piper's shoulder. "You know, I'm feeling an attack of guilt coming on. Because . . . we haven't exactly been the most supportive mates lately."

Piper looked down, then looked at Phoebe skeptically.

"I mean, the whole experience with Josh made me realize how perfect Cole is for me," Phoebe said. "He respects my magic, instead of fearing it. He's never run away from the challenge of Halliwell life."

Phoebe's voice choked.

"And I was going to tell him all this, as soon as things calmed down," she continued. "Now, I just hope I get the chance."

"You're right," Piper said, slumping against the kitchen island. "Those dumb quizzes. Why did I think my marriage was in a rut?"

Suddenly Piper turned to Paige.

"You're right," she said. "This is probably the sappiest thing you'll ever hear me say, but . . . maybe love can conquer all. Or at least, Lupercalus. So let's give it a shot."

Throwing open the basement door, Piper quickly put every growling guy in the room in freeze frame. Then Paige hurried down to the bottom of the stairs, where Leo was frozen in midscowl. She orbed him into the kitchen. Once the basement door was securely locked again, Piper nodded at Paige and Phoebe. They maneuvered Leo into a chair. Then each grabbed one of his arms.

Finally Piper flicked her finger at her husband, unfreezing him.

"Piper!" Leo roared. Instantly, his right hand sprouted razor nails and he began flailing, struggling to break free of Phoebe and Paige's grip.

"Leo . . ." Piper began.

"Sorry . . . you'll be *sorry*!" Leo yelled.

"Stop it!" Piper cried. She dropped to her

knees in front of Leo. Suddenly she forgot all about the plan. It was as if the crisis—and her sisters—had melted away. And it was just she and Leo here in the kitchen, the way they'd been so many times, hanging out, chatting, laughing about Piper's culinary experiments.

Why did I never appreciate those things until they were nearly gone, Piper thought, tears springing to her eyes.

"Leo," Piper began, "I'm sorry for what I've put you through the last few days. I don't know what I was thinking. Those things that might make you a less-than-ideal modern husband, according to some clueless relationship guru . . . those are the things that make you mine. I love how you won't let me open a door, no matter how strong my magic is. I love the way you wake me up every morning with a goofy little song. I love that you're content, Leo."

As Piper spoke, feeling like every word was coming from some untapped well in her heart, she saw her husband's face begin to soften.

Glancing hesitantly at Phoebe, Piper placed a tender hand on Leo's knee.

"Okay, so you're quirky," she said with a small smile. "Having a husband who's, well, dead has its challenges. But it also means—I'm living with an angel. I'll never take that for granted again."

With that, Piper slowly leaned in. She was sure she saw a flicker of recognition in Leo's eyes just before their lips connected in a soft, adoring kiss.

Piper pulled back and smiled sweetly at Leo. The moment was so blissful, she'd forgotten her sisters were even there. She was startled when Phoebe whispered, "He's calmed down. I think it worked!"

Shakily, Piper stood up. She gazed at Leo's face, which was locked in a dreamy smile. Then she looked at Paige and Phoebe.

"Let him go," she said.

"Are you sure—"

"Let him go," Piper said. "He's my husband. I know Leo will never hurt me."

Tentatively, Phoebe and Paige released Leo's arms. He stood shakily and took a halting step toward Piper. It wasn't until he'd almost reached her that Piper glanced down and noticed . . . Leo's clawed hand. It hadn't returned to normal.

"Um, Leo? . . ." she squeaked.

"Who's sorry now, woman?" Leo roared, raising his talons over his head.

Chapter

11

"Okay, that didn't work!" Paige screamed as Leo moved in on Piper, ready to rip her heart out. Phoebe leapt onto her brother-in-law. She straddled his back and grabbed his flailing claw.

"Piper," she yelled. "Freeze him!"

Piper had stumbled backward into the middle of the kitchen. She stared at Leo, who was spinning around, trying to fight Phoebe off. She was in a daze. She couldn't believe her outpouring of love had had no effect on her husband.

"Leo, please," she cried, broadcasting all the hurt she felt into that one word.

Leo stopped fighting Phoebe for an instant. His eyes connected with Piper's. She gasped in hope.

And then, with a great burst of strength, he heaved Phoebe off of him, sending her flying onto the kitchen table.

Without another moment's hesitation Piper threw up her hands and froze her husband in his tracks. Paige pointed at the frozen Leo and orbed him into the basement. Unfortunately she accidentally orbed the raging Alan *out* of the basement at the same time.

"Yah!" Alan cried, ducking and rolling behind the kitchen island before any of the sisters could get a handle on him.

Paige grabbed a meat mallet out of the ceramic pitcher of kitchen tools Piper kept by the stove. Phoebe sent Piper a silent signal with her eyes. Phoebe snuck around one side of the island and Piper around the other.

One, Piper mouthed.

"Two," Phoebe whispered.

"Three!" Paige screeched.

But when all three sisters pounced to the opposite side of the island, Alan was nowhere to be seen.

"Um, screaming sort of does away with the element of surprise we so value," Phoebe said to Paige, rolling her eyes.

"Sorry," Paige said. "This whole ambush thing is a little new to me. I got overexcited."

"And for that," said a sinister male voice above them, "you'll pay!"

Piper gasped as she glanced at the stove. Perched like an agile monkey on the hood over the range was Alan, his silver claws glinting in the afternoon sunlight that flooded the kitchen.

"How did he do that?" Paige demanded.

"Something tells me there's more to Lupercalus's magic than meets the eye," Phoebe said.

"Yeah?" Piper said, still seething over Leo's rejection. "Well, two can play at that."

And before she could stop herself, she flicked her fingers at Alan. He leapt from the stove hood just before an explosion blasted a black, smoky hole in the white-enameled tin.

He landed on the desk chair, crouched like a feral cat. Piper promptly shot another blast at him. He dove out of the way again and this time, it was the computer printer that bit it, exploding in a shower of sparks.

"Piper!" Phoebe cried. "Remember? Innocent? We've got to subdue him without, you know, *subduing* him!"

Piper's hands halted in midflick.

Phoebe dashed across the kitchen and caught Alan in the gut with a neat roundhouse kick. Then she pummeled him across the floor, backing him up until he was standing in front of the basement door, woozily trying to fend off Phoebe's blows.

"Someone get the door!" Phoebe grunted. Piper rushed over and opened the door a crack. Phoebe shoved him through it, then slammed the door in his sneering face.

"Oh my God," Piper said shakily as Phoebe slid the lock into place. "What did I almost do?"

"It's okay," Phoebe said. "Piper, you're only human."

"Half-human," Piper corrected her. "My witch half should be above revenge. It's like I've been infected by Lupercalus too. No offense, Paige."

Piper glanced at Paige. She was staring at the obliterated printer with her fingers to her chin.

"Paige?" Piper said again. "Hello? You there?"

"The computer," Paige said softly. "That's how he did it."

"What?" Phoebe said, walking over to Paige.

"It all connects," Paige said, staring at her sisters. "I can't believe I didn't see it. Lupercalus got into my head through the computer!"

"Okay, back up," Piper said. She righted the desk chair that had somehow survived her little fire fight with Alan. Then she sat Paige down. "Start at the beginning."

"Okay, well, I remember when I was clicking through Kiss.com—every time I clicked the mouse, these little flashes would pop out of the screen," Paige said as Phoebe and Piper pulled up chairs to sit next to her. "They made me feel a bit dizzy. Then I forgot all about it."

"Oh-kay," Piper said. "Go on."

"Well, here's the thing," Paige said. "Max made me feel dizzy too. In the same way that the computer did. I figured I was lovesick. But maybe it was his icky demon-ness messing with my head."

"Hang on," Phoebe said. "This sounds familiar. I'm going to snag the Book of Shadows."

A few minutes later, Phoebe had the Book open on the kitchen counter. And she was pointing at a page in triumph.

"I knew it," she declared. "This is a section about different classes of demons. It says ephemeral demons can exist in the earth's orbit, electrical fields, nuclear power sources—anything that retains energy."

"That explains why Max's weapons were such shockers," Piper said. "He's made of electricity!"

"And to become corporeal and do his dirty work," Phoebe continued, squinting at the Book of Shadows, "the demon needs a magic conduit."

"And what is a witch-slash-Whiteligher if not magic, incorporated?" Piper said. "So Lupercalus was lurking within Kiss.com, waiting for someone both lovelorn and supernatural to click in."

"Oh, this is *so* embarrassing," Paige said, dropping her head into her hands.

Phoebe slammed the Book shut and hopped off the counter.

"Would it make you feel any better if I told you about the time we turned into the seven deadly sins?" Phoebe said. "And mine was lust?"

"Oh, yeah," Piper said. "Now *that* was embarrassing."

"Well, at least I didn't max out all our credit cards with my *greed*," Phoebe said, sneering playfully at Piper. "Talk about embarrassing. Paige, she literally bought a George Foreman grill for every room in the house."

"Okay, let's stick to the subject, shall we?" Piper cut in. "Here's my hunch. Lupercalus was exiled in the computer until Paige's presence released him. So the way to get rid of him?"

She pointed at the darkened computer screen.

"We need to keep him out of the box."

Half an hour later Phoebe was putting the final touches on a spell while Piper paced in front of the basement door.

"We have to hurry," she said. "The natives are definitely getting restless down there."

No sooner had the words left her mouth than a loud crash reverberated out of the basement.

"Sorry!!!!" several of the possessed men bellowed in response.

"Yeah," Piper yelled at the door. "Say it like you mean it."

She turned to her sisters.

"Who knew revenge demons were so darn tedious!" she said.

"Okay!" Phoebe announced, finishing her spell with a flourish. "Plan in place. All we have to do is get Lupercalus into the kitchen and engage him in a fight, which should be easy enough, considering his violent tendencies.

Then when he hurls one of his energy balls, Piper freezes it. I douse the ball with the Origin potion, which we will be whipping up shortly, and it will zing right back into him, hopefully knocking him out of his corporeal state. Then, while he's still all fizzy, we say the spell that will whoosh him into our low-tech receptacle."

Phoebe held up a thick, glass mason jar with a vacuum-seal top.

"Grams's pickles lasted for decades in this thing," she said. "And it's about as nonelectronic as you can get. So it ought to hold Lupercalus— indefinitely."

"*Not* the simplest solution we've ever had to work with," Piper said, biting her lip. "But, I've got to say, it works."

"Except for one little glitch," Phoebe suddenly realized. "We can't do any of this stuff without our handy-dandy demon in hand. Now that Max knows we're onto him, and he's got a veritable army of heartsuckers shacked up in our basement, why would he come back on his own?"

"I guess," Piper said with a sigh, "we're going to have to play fetch-the-demon. Which means someone's going to have to make another trip down that silver rabbithole."

"Ugh," Phoebe said, slapping her hands together wearily. "Time to pummel a portal out of another suitor. Let's move all the breakables out of the room this time."

• • •

A half hour later Paige and Phoebe were hurtling through a brand-new, gooey time portal, which had emerged from the head of the first suitor Paige orbed in—Alan, as luck would have it.

"Beggars can't be choosers," Phoebe had said as she gave Alan a swift belt across the jaw. That had been enough to unleash another howling cyclone. And, gripping each other's hands tightly, Paige and Phoebe had jumped in. Piper stayed home to give Alan his memory spell and brew up the Origin potion they'd need to banish Lupercalus. She'd promised to wait exactly an hour, then say the "Wytch Summoning" spell that would bring them back through the portal, hopefully with Lupercalus as their hostage.

Squelch!

After a long, circuitous tumble, the tunnel finally spat Paige and Phoebe out. Paige bounced, screaming, across a hard surface, then stood up rubbing her backside painfully.

"Ew!" she said. "That was the most disgusting trip of my life."

"That's time travel for you," Phoebe said. She'd landed right next to Paige with a painful yelp. Then she stood up and flicked a stream of silvery goo off her arm.

"But at least this time I know exactly where to find our de—"

Phoebe stopped in mid-declaration and looked around in a panic.

"Uh . . . Paige?" she said, looking around her wildly. "Does this look like ancient Alexandria to you?"

"Not unless there was a lost civilization of Soho in ancient Egypt," Paige said, gazing at the apartment in which they'd landed, complete with exposed rafters, twelve-foot ceilings, and giant windows with a gorgeous, urban view. "This is the coolest loft I've ever seen!"

"Well, would you expect anything less of Max Wolf, superlawyer and revenge demon?" Phoebe said. "Be on your guard, Paige."

"Good point," Paige said, walking slowly across the red-tinted cement floor. She paused by the long, glass dining-room table with the black leather-and-chrome chairs. In the middle of the table was a black vase containing one perfect calla lily. Across an Oriental rug was a gleaming open kitchen and, beyond that, a Chinese screen hiding . . . something. Paige gave Phoebe a hard look, then nodded at the screen. Together they tiptoed over.

Paige held her breath, then quickly peeked around the screen. She was so sure that Lupercalus would be lying in wait for them, she was almost disappointed to see nothing but a pristine, low bed piled high with a fluffy, white-and-taupe duvet.

"Well, the guy's got impeccable taste, I'll give him that," Phoebe said stepping cautiously into Max's bedroom and glancing around. The loft was clearly empty. "I feel like we've walked into a Crate and Barrel catalog."

Blurp.

"Phoebe?!" Paige cried. She blinked and stared into the bedroom. Phoebe had been walking toward the bed. And then, with a wet, squelching sound she'd disappeared.

Into thin air.

She was just—gone.

"What's going on?" Paige screamed, lurching into the bedroom.

Blurp.

Paige felt as if someone had just pushed her through a wall of Jell-O. And when she emerged, the illusion continued. She was floating in a substance, a crystal-clear, bright blue gel.

And there was Phoebe, floating nearby, looking as shell-shocked as she felt.

"I guess that loft was too good to be true," Phoebe said, her voice sounding burbly and far away in this strange substance.

"I'm just grateful they have oxygen here," Paige said. "Now we need to figure out where 'here' is."

They were surrounded on all sides by flashing yellow lights and glowing bars. Slashes of lightning occasionally zapped over their heads or below their feet. And in the distance, Paige could see a tall rectangular structure that looked eerily familiar.

"What is that?" Paige said, pointing at the huge structure.

"Is it a building?" Phoebe replied hopefully.

Paige made swimming motions and was surprised to feel herself zing through the blue gel, leaving a bubbly wake behind her. Phoebe swam up next to her, then whizzed ahead.

"I've got to admit," Paige said, feeling the cool, gelatinous substance skim over her skin. "This stuff is kind of cool."

Suddenly, Phoebe threw her arms out to the side, bringing herself to a startled halt. The "building" they'd been swimming toward had just come into view. Paige followed Phoebe's gaze.

"I know what that is," Paige said. "It's a . . . a . . ."

"Computer chip," Phoebe said. "It's a giant computer chip. Actually what's more likely is that the computer chip is a normal size, which means we've been shrunk to the size of pinheads and plopped into Lupercalus's virtual world."

"Oh," Paige said flatly. "Well . . . *this* is new. But definitely not improved. You think the spell to bring us back will still work from here, don't you?"

"I don't see why not," Phoebe said, spinning around and scanning the bizarre electriworld for Lupercalus. "Not that it'll do us any good if we haven't bagged our demon by then."

"Right," Paige said, looking at her watch. "And we only have fourteen minutes to do it before Piper calls us home."

"Well," Phoebe said, gazing into the empty abyss. "I'm stumped. He could be anywhere or anything down here. He might have returned to his ephemeral state, in which case, he'd be invisible."

"So . . . as your Grams likes to say," Paige suggested, "get him! Write a spell. Just start rhyming."

"A spell?" Phoebe said. "Just off the top of my head? Just like that? Paige, I don't think you understand how delicate an operation spell-wri—"

"Give us this soul, um, brimming with malice . . ." Paige called out. "Bring before us, Lupercalus!"

"*That's* your spell?" Phoebe said with a patronizing smile. "Well, it's not bad—"

"What the *hell* is going on here!"

Phoebe and Paige whirled around in the bubbly gel to see . . . the demon himself.

Lupercalus was floating before them.

His hair had morphed from his slicked do into a long, flowing mane. He'd ditched his earth clothes and was clad in a shimmery, silver robe. And his yellow eyes were glowing bright with rage.

"No witch has the power to summon me in

my own world," Lupercalus raged. His face was a mask of anger and just a hint of confusion.

"No *mere* witch," Paige countered. "But, Lupercalus, you should have done a bit of research before possessing *this* witch. We're the Charmed Ones."

"And guess who's gonna be sorry, now?" Phoebe said. She kicked her legs and whipped over to Lupercalus, putting his head in a choke hold.

"Off!" Lupercalus bellowed. His entire body began to spark and he zapped Phoebe with a lightning bolt of pain. Moaning, she released him and floated backward. Her arms trembled violently.

Paige gasped and backed away as Lupercalus took a moment to recover. Then he began to float toward her, his eyes narrowing to gold slits. Paige gave him a defiant glare, then glanced quickly at her watch. She gasped when she saw the time.

"Phoebe," Paige said, catching her sister's eye. "Thirty seconds."

"I'm on it," Phoebe gasped.

"On what?" Lupercalus sneered. "Do you really think you can conquer me? And in my own environment? You know, my demons aren't the only ones who have claws."

With that, Lupercalus raised both hands in the air. Almost instantly each hand morphed into a network of gnashing blades. His weapons were twice as foreboding as those of his possessed minions.

Phoebe shot Paige a terrified glance.

Five seconds, Paige mouthed, glancing at her digital watch. *Four . . . three . . .*

"You know, Max," Phoebe said as she neatly dodged a swipe of Lupercalus's hand. "Great knives. But bad timing." She leapt upon him from behind, grabbing both wrists and yanking them behind his head. Lupercalus roared in rage, but, for that instant anyway, did seem to be paralyzed by Phoebe's strength.

Then Phoebe squeezed her eyes shut and waited for the portal to emerge. She could picture Piper in the kitchen, uttering the spell, her potion in hand. *Piper always comes through*, Phoebe thought gratefully.

The only glitch in the warm fuzzy? The portal never came.

Chapter

12

Half an hour after Paige and Phoebe leapt into the time portal, Piper had sent a confused but memory-washed Alan on his way. Then she'd placed the mason jar and its quick-seal top carefully on the kitchen's island.

Now she was nervously putting the finishing touches on the Origin spell, and just in time. She only had five minutes before she had to read the spell that would summon Phoebe, Paige, and hopefully, their revenge demon, back into the kitchen.

Piper tossed exactly five mustard seeds into the bubbling saucepan on the stove, then looked at her watch.

"And three, two, one—"

Boom!

A pink geyser erupted out of the pot like a garish flower. Then it plopped back into the potion.

"Okay," Piper muttered, peering into the Book of Shadows. "Next it should turn 'brackish green, then corpse blue.' Ugh, potions like this are what give witches a bad name. We couldn't describe them, say, as *mossy* green and *powder* blue?"

Piper watched as her bubbly potion began to change color.

"Well, at least it's working," she said. "And I've got to admit, 'corpse blue' is the perfect description for that color."

She took another peek at her recipe.

"Now add . . . well, what do you know!" Piper said, reading the recipe again. "Eye of newt! I thought it was just a myth. But there actually *is* a potion that calls for eye of newt!"

Paige sifted through Grams's old spice box and found a dusty glass bottle filled with tiny, black orbs. Cringing she popped two of the tiny eyeballs into her palm, then dropped them into the pot.

She let the potion simmer for thirty more seconds, then used her turkey baster (which would no longer be used for turkey, that was for sure) to transfer the potion into a glass vial. Piper corked it up and checked her watch.

"Perfect," she said, slipping the vial into her capri pants pocket. "Made it with one minute to spare."

She walked around the island with the Book of Shadows and flipped to the page with the summoning spell.

And that's when the basement door splintered and three, glinting, clawed hands thrust themselves into the kitchen.

"Oh, great!" Piper cried, dropping the Book on the floor. "*Now* you guys figure out how to work together? I don't have time for this!"

She hurried to the door, getting ready to freeze the demons before they could bust into the kitchen. But just as she reached the door, it crashed open, hitting her square in the chest.

"Ooof!" Piper grunted as the blow threw her through the air. She heard, rather than felt, her head hit the kitchen island.

Leo, she thought, her eyelids fluttering weakly, *help me.*

And then she felt her consciousness slip away into gray, followed by total darkness.

"Phoebe?" Paige said through gritted teeth. "Where's the portal?"

"Search me!" Phoebe grunted.

"If only I had a free hand, I would," Paige replied with a grimace.

But every one of the sisters' limbs was occupied in trying to overpower Lupercalus and his thrashing, lethal hands. The three of them were still suspended in virtual, blue gel, and entangled in one brutal battle.

And the demon had the advantage.

"You'll never take me," Lupercalus raged, spinning around in the computer-generated gel.

"After all, an ethereal demon can take all forms," he continued.

And that's when Max Wolf began to melt away. His handsome, rugged face began to morph into a reptilian visage—green, slimy, and encrusted with raw scabs. His yellow eyes bulged like those of a corpse. His body began to elongate. Slipping out of his silvery robe, Lupercalus became a slimy, eel-like, seven-foot-long . . . monster.

Paige and Phoebe took one look at each other. Then both of them screamed the same thing: "Piper!"

But when their screams subsided, the substance in which they were floating became eerily silent.

Okay, Paige thought in panic, *our time portal? It's definitely not happening. As an alternative, my new boyfriend is going to eat us!*

Paige grabbed Phoebe's hand and mouthed to her, *What now?*

Lupercalus was swimming around them in a predatory circle. He flicked his thick, scaly tail, sending a froth of bubbles into their faces. Then he reared back and spat at them. But instead of something wet and slimy, Lupercalus spat electricity. A sparking energy ball whizzed past Phoebe's ear.

"I've created this world!" Lupercalus roared. "I control it. Which means I control you! And believe me, I'll have some fun with you before I kill you."

"Just like you did with Catherine!" Phoebe yelled.

Ooh, Paige thought as Lupercalus skidded to a halt and roared with rage. *Perhaps that wasn't the most tactful way to put it.*

"Never mind, then," he said to Phoebe. "If that's what you want, I'll just slay you now."

"Phoebe!" Paige screamed. She began to hyperventilate as Lupercalus reared back and opened his mouth wide. His teeth were long and jagged and they were stained a disgusting brown.

Phoebe grabbed Paige by the shoulders and stared at her fiercely.

"Orb!" she ordered her.

"What?" Paige gasped.

"Paige, orb us out of here," Phoebe said. "Get us home or we're doomed."

"My orbing, it's so haphazard, I don't know—"

"Now, Paige!" Phoebe screamed. Then she turned to Lupercalus and shouted, "You want us? Come and get us!"

"*Raaaaaggghhh!*" Lupercalus screeched. He lunged at the sisters in full attack mode.

"Aaaagggh!" Paige screamed.

She grabbed Phoebe. And then she orbed.

When the white lights shimmered away, Paige blinked and looked around. They were no longer floating in blue gel and Lupercalus was nowhere to be seen. She heaved a shaky sigh of relief.

Then she stopped for a minute to regard her surroundings: big, green, leafy stalks. A cloudless blue sky. And a rustly, peaceful breeze.

Mooooo.

And . . . the sound of a cow nearby.

"Uh-oh," Paige said.

"Paige," Phoebe said, shielding her eyes and looking around. "This . . . is a cornfield. I think you orbed us to Iowa."

"Well, Iowa's better than Lupercalus's hologram from hell, isn't it?" Paige protested. "I told you, my orbing isn't quite refined yet."

"Well, you'd better get it refined, because I just baited Lupercalus into following us!" Phoebe shrieked. "And if he took the bait, then he's probably making an appearance at Halliwell Manor right about now."

"Piper!" Paige breathed. She grabbed Phoebe's hand and squeezed her eyes shut. She tried to envision Halliwell Manor, to propel herself through the heavens and make a direct hit to her new home. She felt the warm, glimmery sensation of her white lights swirling around her body. She felt the weightless zoom of the orb. And then she opened her eyes.

"Close, but no banana, Paige!" Phoebe was screaming.

Paige found herself clutching a metal beam and fighting a whipping wind. She looked down and saw a stream of tiny cars, and then, a swirling body of water.

"The Golden Gate bridge?!?" Paige squeaked. "I orbed us onto the top of the Golden Gate?"

"Yup!" Phoebe cried from her awkward perch on a nearby beam. "And I'm losing my grip. Try again!"

Paige reached out for her sister and orbed as soon as she felt their fingertips touch. When the white lights finished fluttering, Paige opened her eyes fearfully.

"Yes!" she cried. She and Phoebe had landed in the Halliwells' kitchen. "I can't believe I did— Piper!?!"

Paige gasped as she saw Piper sprawled on the kitchen floor. The Book of Shadows was lying next to her. She was out cold.

"Phoebe, help me get Piper into the living room," Paige said, rushing over to her unconscious sister.

"Um," Phoebe quavered, "now is not the best time."

Paige looked up in confusion and saw Phoebe backing away from a phalanx of men—Teddy, Charlie, James, and Cole. Their eyes had begun to glow yellow, just like Lupercalus's. And they were swinging their clawed hands malevolently.

"Little help here?" Phoebe squeaked.

"Mallet!" Paige cried, feeling a surge of heat in her hand as the wooden meat mallet orbed into it. Then she stole up behind the quartet of possessed men and gave each one a swift thwack on the head. Like a stack of dominoes, they each crumpled to the floor.

Paige stared at the pile of men and wondered out loud, "Where's Leo?"

"No time to look," Phoebe said, turning to Piper. She ran to her pale, limp sister and leaned over her. And that's when a familiar howling filled the kitchen.

Paige and Phoebe clutched each other as a time portal erupted gushily from the floor. Its mouth pulsated and glowed, shooting little lightning bolts into the kitchen.

"Ow!" Paige screamed as a searing bolt of electricity grazed her arm. It sent a jolt of hot pain down to her wrist *and* burned a hole in her favorite silk cardigan. She glanced at Phoebe.

"Well, I guess your bait worked," she yelled over the roaring of the portal's swirl of wind. "But now what do we do? With Piper laid out, we don't have the Power of Three. And I don't see the Origin potion anywhere. Maybe Piper didn't have a chance to make it!"

"Piper!" Phoebe said, roughly shaking her sister by the shoulders. "Oh, please, Piper, we need you!"

"You'll need all the help you can get," roared a demonic voice. Phoebe and Paige whipped around and screamed as Lupercalus, still in his crusty, slimy, monster-eel body, slithered out of the time portal. Immediately the portal closed and melted away into nothingness, which left the demon alone, in the middle of the Halliwells' kitchen. His bald, scaly head hit the ceiling, leaving dents in the plaster as he skimmed across the floor to thrust his face into Paige's. His breath was hot and smelled of an electrical fire.

"You wanted love, did you?" he cried. "Well, *I* wanted love too. I offered Catherine a kingdom. But unfortunately for you she rejected me. Out of spite. Out of malice."

"You don't know what love is, you monster," Paige sneered.

"Then . . . neither will you," Lupercalus bellowed. He opened his mouth wide and lunged for Paige's neck. She screamed and braced herself for death.

But instead she felt a shoe graze the tip of her nose as Phoebe cut in, kicking Lupercalus square in the jaw. Brown, rotten teeth scattered onto the floor and the demon howled in pain, stumbling backward. Paige threw herself against his gut and gave a tremendous push. The already off-balance monster collapsed, pinning his own tail beneath him. A lightning bolt burst out of his mouth as he hit the floor.

"I've got him," Phoebe said, pouncing on Lupercalus with a volley of kicks, punches, and stomps. "Try to revive Piper!"

"Okay," Paige said breathlessly, stumbling away from the fight and turning to her other sister. But somebody was already leaning over her.

Somebody with matted blond hair and a wild look in his eyes.

"Leo!" Paige screamed. "Nooooo!"

Imagining Leo's morphed, knifelike fingers digging into Piper's chest, Paige leapt across the kitchen and pounced on him. But he barely moved, so focused was he on his wife.

"Stop it!" Paige screamed, grabbing at Leo's arm.

But her mouth clapped shut as soon as she saw what Leo was *actually* doing. He wasn't piercing Piper's flesh with his silver nails. In fact his talons weren't even bared. Instead he was resting his palms on Piper's head and they were glowing brightly.

An instant later Piper's eyes fluttered open.

"Leo, you're back?" Piper said.

"I'm back," Leo said. "I don't know what happened. I saw you lying there and it was like something shut off in my brain. Something terrible. Oh, Piper, I'm so sorry I tried to hurt you!"

"It wasn't you, sweetie," Piper said, wrapping her arms around her husband. "It wasn't you. I know that."

Over Leo's shoulder, Piper saw Paige. Her eyes widened.

"Paige!" she exclaimed, disentangling herself from her husband's embrace. "How did you get here? Did I say the spell? And, oh my God, what is that thing?"

Piper was pointing at Lupercalus, who was

still locked in battle with Phoebe. He was matching her blow for blow, and literally spitting fire. Both witch and demon were screaming with rage. But only Phoebe was growing weak. Paige could see her already beginning to stumble.

"Never mind how we got back here," Paige said. "It's spell-time again. Piper, did you make the potion?"

Piper reached into her pants pocket and pulled out a glass vial of blue liquid. Paige grabbed it and called out to Phoebe.

"Phoebe, over here!"

Then she turned to Leo and pointed at the pile of comatose suitors near the breakfast table.

"Orb those guys out of here, will you?" she said. "I don't want them to get hurt."

As Leo cleared the room with a flurry of white lights, Phoebe glanced over her shoulder. She saw Paige and Piper standing next to each other by the stove and leapt away from Lupercalus. She stumbled over to her sisters. Piper put an arm around Phoebe, who was almost too exhausted to stand after her knockout fight with the demon.

But the demon, of course, was ready for more.

"Three little maids, all in a row," he roared. "The better to obliterate you all at once."

He reared back and hawked with a disgusting, wretching noise. Then he spat a giant blue ball of shimmering sparks across the room.

Paige uncorked the vial of Origin potion. Cringing, she threw the ice blue liquid through the air. The energy ball and potion collided over the island with a violent, hissing noise.

"Oooh, I hope this works," Phoebe cried.

The energy ball was definitely halted by the potion. It hovered in the air for a moment, sizzling and shooting little lightning bolts in all directions.

And then, slowly, the ball reversed direction.

"What the—" Lupercalus began. But then the energy ball made a direct hit. Screeching in terror and pain, Lupercalus's demonic shape exploded with a huge, mind-blowing boom.

The sisters ducked and covered their heads, expecting a slime bath. But all that came of the explosion was a huge poof of shimmery, silvery dust, pulsing in the air like a swarm of supernatural bees.

"The spell!" Piper cried, pulling a slip of paper from her pocket. "All together!"

The Halliwells began to chant as one:

Lupercalus, vengeful soul,
We bind you from your evil goal.
Through Catherine's will
And our Charmed power
Let this be your last cruel hour.

As the last word echoed through the room, the shimmering swarm began to vibrate and writhe. Then the cloud seemed to recoil. It was trying to fight off a force that was sucking it in. But Lupercalus—ephemeral and helpless once again—was no match for the Charmed Ones' magic. The swirl of dust became compact as it began to shoot into the mason jar on the kitchen counter. As the last specks popped into the jar, a horrible howl filled the house, a scream of agony and frustration. It was one last, fruitless call for revenge.

Piper popped the top on the mason jar and twisted it until the vacuum-seal gave a little pop.

Then all was quiet.

As Paige and Phoebe slumped over in exhaustion, Piper grabbed a permanent marker and a label out of the desk drawer.

"Revenge Demon—Do Not Open—EVER!" she wrote on the label before sticking it onto the jar. Then, without ceremony, she went to the pantry and tucked the dust-filled mason jar onto the back of the highest shelf.

"And that, as they say in the tennis world, is a match," Piper said, turning to her sisters with a weary smile. "Halliwells, forty. Lupercalus, love."

Epilogue

Phoebe tiptoed into the bedroom where Cole was sleeping and got to work. She placed a huge, foil-wrapped chocolate kiss on the nightstand. Then she scattered red rose petals all over the comforter. Next she poured a cup of Cole's favorite French roast coffee into a mug and wafted it beneath his nose.

Bingo. The boy was rising.

"Phoebe?" he said groggily. He blinked sleepily and raised his head off the pillow. "What time is it?"

"It's Valentine's Day, that's what time it is," Phoebe announced. She planted a sloppy kiss on Cole's forehead. "Which leads us to a very serious question: Will you be my Valentine, Mr. Turner?"

Cole gave Phoebe a sly grin and said, "Only if you'll be mine, Ms. Halliwell."

"Drink," Phoebe ordered, thrusting the fragrant mug of joe beneath his nose. "I know you can't be taken at your word until you've had your A.M. caffeine. Then again neither can I. Can I have a sip?"

Cole took a loud slurp of coffee, then passed the mug to Phoebe. He scooped a handful of rose petals off the bedspread and sprinkled them playfully over her head.

"Hey, you're ruining the romantic set design," Phoebe protested with a laugh.

Cole laughed too. Then his face darkened a bit and he pulled Phoebe into his arms.

"Phoebe, are you really sure this is what you want?"

"Being your Valentine?" Phoebe asked, still grinning.

"Being my fiancée," Cole said. "The whole Lupercalus episode . . . well, it was a bit illuminating."

Phoebe looked down guiltily.

"I never did tell you what happened with Josh in ancient Egypt," she said. "But I want to tell you now."

Phoebe felt Cole stiffen. His blue eyes went steely as he said, "Okay, I'm ready to hear it."

"Josh finally explained to me what went wrong in our relationship," Phoebe said. "While we witnessed Maxentius putting Saint Catherine through torture, we had a little torture of our own: Revisiting the past."

"And . . ." Cole asked, his jaw clenching.

"And I realized what our problem was," Phoebe said, cupping Cole's cheeks in her hands. "He wasn't you. Cole, I'm so grateful to have you. Not only because you're strong and smart and a total babe but because . . . you're not afraid to marry a psychic, levitating, butt-kicking witch who's very, very close with her sisters."

"Now that you put it that way," Cole said, "um, I think I have to leave!"

"You!" Phoebe giggled, giving him a swat on the arm.

"Seriously, though," Cole said, "I'm not just grateful for you, Phoebe. I'm proud of you. Your strength is nothing but good. For me . . . and for us."

There was nothing else Phoebe could say. She could only lean into her sweetie and plant a soft, sweet kiss on his lips.

"Speaking of strength," she murmured as Cole nibbled her earlobe, "mine is waning. Let's sneak down to the kitchen and make a little breakfast picnic."

"Perfect," Cole said.

They tossed on some bathrobes and crept down the stairs.

"Stay quiet," Phoebe whispered over her shoulder as they padded across the dining room to the kitchen. "I love it when we have the place to our—oh, uh, hi guys."

Piper, who was lounging at the kitchen table in her pajamas, jumped. And Leo, who'd been dangling a chocolate-covered strawberry over Piper's lips, went hot pink in the cheeks.

"We caught you being mushy!" Phoebe teased.

"Yeah, happy Valentine's Day to you, too," Piper said, mock-glaring at her sister and Cole.

"I guess we're all in the mood for love, now that we don't have a bitter revenge demon messing with our heads," Phoebe said. As Leo and Cole flopped into a couple of kitchen chairs, she headed to the fridge. She emerged with a bowl of eggs and a stick of butter.

"Of course, none of our heads were messed with as badly as Paige's," Piper said, guiltily. She pulled a loaf of homemade whole-wheat out of the breadbox and started slicing it.

"You're right," Phoebe said. "It's such a bummer. Here she was, looking for love, and instead, she got revenge, death, time travel, demonology . . ."

"There's got to be some cultural message in that," Cole piped up.

"Nah, just the usual trials and tribulations of singleton life," Phoebe said. "Ooh, am I glad it's behind me."

"Really?" Cole said, locking eyes with Phoebe from across the room.

Phoebe abandoned the eggs she was cracking into a bowl and went to sit on Cole's lap.

"Really!" she assured him, giving him a kiss on the cheek.

"Now, now, enough with the PDA," Piper said. "I think we should try to be sensitive to Paige today. The whole reason she went on Kiss.com was to find a Valentine's sweetie. So she might be really bummed this morning."

"*Good* morning to you, too!" Paige said. She'd just popped through the door. She practically bounced into the kitchen. "What's for breakfast, Ma?"

"Oh, how about omelets, Biff," Piper said, scanning Paige's face for angst. How much of that had she heard?

"Cool," Paige said, sitting in a chair next to Cole and Phoebe. "Can you make mine first? I've got to take off in a few minutes."

"No prob," Piper said, taking over the breakfast prep from Phoebe as usual.

Chime.

"Ugh, the dreaded doorbell," Phoebe said, shivering as she slid off Cole's lap into a chair of her own. "Ever since Paige's dates from hell, I hate that sound."

"Um, Phoebe," Piper said through gritted teeth. She pointed her eggy whisk at her sister threateningly. "Remember what I said about, you know, *sensitivity*?"

But Paige was oblivious.

"I'll get it!" she sing-songed, dashing out of the room.

"Well, for someone who's romantically crushed, Paige is pretty cheery!" Phoebe said. "And what's she wearing? A sparkly tube top and miniskirt? That's a little racy for work clothes. Even for Paige!"

"Well, maybe I'm not going straight to work," Paige announced, re-entering the kitchen with a triumphant grin. Spilling out of her arms were three bouquets of flowers.

"Who are those from?" Piper gasped.

"I don't know, let's see!" Paige said with a grin. She sifted through the pink roses and frothy hydrangeas, fishing out three cards.

"Aw, Just James," she said, reading one. "Such a doll. And Teddy remembered how much I like sweet peas. And who's this weird-looking one from? Oh! Lung Chow!"

"Paige?" Phoebe said. "I'm confused. Weren't your dates total duds?"

"They were, but now they're studs!" Paige said. "You guys were right. Lupercalus totally hexed me. When I gave the guys another chance, and, more importantly, they gave me one, I found each one more irresistible than the last."

"Did she say, 'fast'?" Leo muttered with a grin.

"I'll pretend I didn't hear that because I have to leave," Paige said, sticking her tongue out at Leo and grinning. Then she went to the walk-in pantry and dug out Sweetie's cat carrier.

"Sweetie!" she called. "Time for your check-up!"

Sweetie, who must have thought Paige was talking about food, trotted into the kitchen. Paige wiggled the skinny Siamese into the cat carrier and snapped the door shut.

"And can I ask where you're going with our familiar?" Phoebe said.

"To the vet," Paige said innocently. "Just a little check-up. No spaying, I promise."

"And would this vet happen to be a red-haired cutie?" Piper said.

"A red-haired Kisser," Phoebe corrected her.

"Let's just say," Paige responded, picking up the cat carrier and sashaying to the door, "that this year, I'm having a charmed Valentine's Day."